Contents

Forever Promised	1
Chapter One: Coming Home	3
Chapter Two: The Cracks Begin to Show	9
Chapter Three: A Promise to Herself	15
Chapter Four: The Cracks Deepen	21
Chapter Five: The Truth Presses In	28
Chapter Six: When the Walls Close In	35
Chapter Seven: The Weight of Truth	40
Chapter Eight: The Unavoidable Truth	45
Chapter Nine: Embracing the Inevitable	51
Chapter Ten: Holding On, Letting Go	56
Chapter Eleven: The Fragility of Time	62
Chapter Twelve: Promises in the Time We Have	68
Chapter Thirteen: The Proposal	78
Chapter Fourteen: In Light and Love	87
Chapter Fifteen: The Weight and Wonder of Love	96
Chapter Sixteen: One Glorious Night	108
Chapter Seventeen: The Promise	117

Chapter Eighteent: The List	128
Chapter Ninteen: Slowing Time	138
Chapter Twenty: What Love Does	149
Chapter Twenty-One: The Deepest Kind of Love	160
Chapter Twenty-Two: The Last Page	169
Chapter Twenty-Three: The Last Sunrise	179

Forever Promised

Katrina Case

Copyright © 2025 Katrina Case

All rights reserved. No part of this book may be reproduced, stored in a retrieval system, or transmitted in any form or by any means—electronic, mechanical, photocopying, recording, or otherwise—without prior written permission from the publisher, except for brief quotations in reviews or academic purposes.

This is a work of fiction. Names, characters, places, and incidents are products of the author's imagination or are used fictitiously. Any resemblance to actual persons, living or dead, events, or locales is entirely coincidental.

Publisher: Literary Reflections
For permissions, inquiries, or more information, contact:
  https://literaryreflections.com

Chapter One: Coming Home

The highway stretched long and empty before Naomi Andrews, a thin silver ribbon weaving through endless miles of open land. It should have felt like freedom. But it didn't. With every mile that brought her closer to Cape May, New Jersey, her chest grew tighter, like something unseen was pressing against her ribs. Home. A word that should feel warm. But to her, it was heavy. She had spent years running away, believing that distance could erase the past. But the past wasn't something you could outrun. It was something that lived in you and waited in quiet corners, ready to rise again the moment you returned. She ran her hand through her wavy brown hair in frustration, and tears tried to well in her tired, hazel eyes, but she fought them back to see the sign that announced she was almost home.

CAPE MAY – 10 MILES

Naomi tightened her grip on the steering wheel, her knuckles pale. Almost there. Her stomach churned—not from nerves, but from the sickness curling deep inside her, the unrelenting ache that had become a permanent part of her body. The doctors had called it Stage IV ovarian cancer. She called it a thief. A thief that had come too soon. She exhaled sharply, rolling down the window. The first breath of ocean air hit her instantly, wrapping around her like something familiar, something that had never truly let her go.

As the sun set, bleeding streaks of tangerine and gold rose across the sky. It was beautiful, almost cruelly beautiful. She swallowed hard. How many more sunsets would she get to see? Not enough.

Naomi pulled into the driveway of her childhood home, her hands trembling slightly as she cut the engine. It was exactly as she remembered. The white shutters, the navy blue door, and the porch swing creaked when the wind blew too hard. The flower beds overflowed with wild lavender and white roses, a reminder of how much her mother still cared for and nurtured this place. Naomi let herself sit there for a second, hands resting in her lap. She wasn't ready for this. But then, the front door swung open.

Ruth Andrews stepped onto the porch, her gray cardigan pulled tight around her frame, her eyes sharp and searching. She knew. Naomi hadn't spoken, but her mother knew something was wrong.

"Naomi," she whispered, stepping down onto the front steps.

Her voice held no anger, no accusations. Just a quiet kind of relief—the kind that comes from finally having something back that you thought was lost.

Naomi forced herself to smile. "Hey, Mom."

And then, her mother pulled her in, holding her like she was afraid she would disappear. The moment Naomi felt the warmth of her mother's embrace, something inside her cracked. She squeezed her eyes shut, breathing in the familiar scent of vanilla and chamomile, the way her mother had always smelled. She wasn't ready to say goodbye, but was running out of time.

The clink of silverware against ceramic plates was the only sound filling the kitchen. Naomi sat across from her father, Thomas Andrews, a man of few words but steady hands—the same hands that had built this house, taught her how to fish off the docks, and lifted her onto his shoulders as a child. Now, they rested motionless on the table.

"You didn't tell us you were coming," her mother said, folding her napkin.

Naomi took a slow sip of her tea. "I wanted to surprise you."

Her father's gaze lifted, calm and unreadable.

"How long are you staying?" he asked.

She hesitated for only a moment. "For the summer."

A lie. Summer had always meant forever to her when she was younger. And this would be the last one she would ever have. Ruth smiled softly, brushing a piece of imaginary lint from the table. "Then we have plenty of time to catch up."

Naomi returned the smile, a fragile curve of her lips that felt hollow—another lie crafted to mask the turmoil within. The grandfather clock in the corner of the living room ticked steadily, its rhythmic cadence echoing through the quiet space. Each second seemed to stretch, an unspoken reminder of the words she struggled to voice. She had never felt the weight of time so acutely before, as if each passing moment was a heavy stone lodged in her chest, pressing down with an urgency that threatened to consume her. The air around her was thick with unsaid truths, amplifying her sense of isolation amidst the warmth of the familiar room.

Later that evening, Naomi wandered into town, drawn to a place that had once felt like her sanctuary: The Turning Page Bookstore. As she pushed open the heavy oak door, a delicate bell jingled cheerfully, echoing the warmth of familiarity. The air inside was infused with the comforting scent of aged paper, sweet vanilla candles, and a hint of soft floral notes, evoking a sense of nostalgia that wrapped around her like a favorite blanket. It felt like time stood still for a moment—nothing had changed. The same mahogany bookshelves, polished to a deep luster, lined the walls, sagging slightly under the weight of countless stories. In the corner, the faded reading nook still beckoned with its well-worn armchair, its fabric fraying at the edges, and the sunlight streaming through the window illuminated dust motes dancing in the air. Memories surged within her, pressing against her ribs like a flood of unspoken words and half-forgotten dreams.

"Naomi?"

She turned at the sound of a familiar voice, her heart skipping a beat. Willow Carmichael stood behind the polished oak counter, her wavy chestnut hair catching the soft glow of the overhead lights. Her brown eyes, usually warm and inviting, were now wide with surprise as she took in the sight of her old friend after so long. The scent of freshly brewed coffee and baked goods lingered in the air, wrapping around them like a cozy blanket, as a hint of the bustling café's chatter faded into the background.

Naomi smiled. "Surprise."

Willow didn't hesitate. She came around the counter and pulled her into a tight hug.

"You should have told me you were coming back," Willow murmured. Her voice was warm, but something else was there, something knowing.

Naomi hesitated. "I didn't want to make a big deal out of it."

Willow pulled back, her brows knitting together. "Are you okay?"

Too long of a pause.

Naomi forced a smile. "Yeah. Just… needed a change of scenery."

A lie she was getting too good at telling. Then—a voice from behind her, low and unmistakably familiar.

"Didn't think I'd see you here again."

Her breath hitched in her throat as she turned slowly. There he stood, Graham Jameson, a formidable presence by the towering bookshelves, his arms crossed over a fitted shirt accentuating his lean frame. He observed her with an intensity that made her feel vulnerable and electrified, as if she were a long-forgotten specter summoned back to life. Her heart stumbled in her chest. He appeared as he always had, yet a palpable difference lingered between them. His jawline was more chiseled, a testament to the years that had shaped him, while his shoulders had broadened, adding to his commanding demeanor. Those familiar stormy blue eyes remained, yet they held a more profound, impenetrable quality—hardened like a tempest threatening to unleash.

"You left without a word," he said, his voice steady.

Naomi's throat went dry. "I know."

Graham exhaled sharply, shaking his head. "Why come back now?"

The question lingered in the air, weighted with a gravity far beyond its simple phrasing. He stood there, caught in uncertainty, grappling with the truth that eluded him. He was oblivious that she had returned, not for a reunion, but to deliver her quiet farewell.

She forced another smile. "I just needed some time here, that's all."

Graham studied her, his gaze sharp. "That's all?"

"That's all," she lied.

As he turned and strode away, the evening light casting long shadows across the pavement, she felt a pang of hurt settle in her chest. The way he had narrowed his eyes, skepticism etched across his face, told her he didn't believe her words, not for a second. She could hear the soft rustle of leaves in the gentle breeze, contrasting with the heaviness between them. Deep down, a conflicting wish stirred within her; perhaps it was for him to hold onto that doubt, to remain distant from the truth she dared not reveal.

Chapter Two: The Cracks Begin to Show

Jameson & Co. Woodworks provides the scent of fresh-cut cedar and sawdust hung thick in the air, a familiar weight pressing against Graham Jameson's senses. The rhythmic sound of sanding, chiseling, and the occasional thunk of wood hitting the workbench usually kept his mind focused and steady. But today, his hands worked on autopilot, his thoughts miles away from the shop. The late morning sun poured through the wide-paned windows, dust motes swirling in golden light. The open garage doors let in the salt-tinged breeze from the bay, carrying with it the distant hum of summer—the sounds of a town coming alive with the season.

But Graham wasn't thinking about summer. He was thinking about her. Naomi. He muttered a curse under his breath and pressed the sandpaper harder against the wooden lighthouse figurine he was carving, trying to block out the way her voice still echoed in his head, the way her eyes—hazel, flecked with green—had locked onto his like she was bracing herself for a storm.

"Watch it!" a voice cut through his thoughts. "You're about to sand that thing down to dust."

Graham clenched his jaw. Beck Jameson, his younger brother, stood at the entrance to the shop, arms crossed, a knowing smirk playing on his lips.

Graham set the sandpaper down with a little too much force. "You need something, or are you just here to annoy me?"

Beck stepped inside, boots scuffing against the wooden floor, dust rising around them. He pulled a rag from his back pocket, wiping his hands as he eyed Graham's work.

"You're distracted."

"No, I'm working."

Beck snorted. "No, you're brooding."

Graham exhaled sharply, rolling his shoulders. "Drop it, Beck."

But his brother wasn't going to drop it. He never did.

Beck grabbed a nearby stool and spun it around, straddling it lazily. "So," he said, stretching out the word, "how'd it feel seeing her again?"

Graham picked up the chisel and turned back to his project. "Like something I don't want to feel."

Beck grinned. "You're lying to yourself."

Graham shot him a warning look, but Beck leaned forward, elbows braced against his knees.

"You're sanding the same spot like you're trying to erase something," Beck said, nodding toward the lighthouse figurine in Graham's hands. "Let me guess—Naomi Andrews?"

Graham forced himself to keep his grip loose, not to snap the delicate carving in half.

"I'm not interested."

Beck tilted his head. "You sure about that?"

Graham's grip tightened.

Beck smirked. "Right. That's why you haven't stopped thinking about her since she walked back into town."

Graham didn't respond. Because Beck was right, and that pissed him off.

"She left without a word," Graham said finally, his voice rough, edged with something unresolved. "I'm not giving her a second chance to do it again."

Beck studied him, his smirk fading into something softer. "Maybe she didn't come back for you."

That one hit harder than it should have.

Graham set the lighthouse down carefully and turned toward his brother, his expression blank. "Good," he said evenly. "I don't need her to."

But the words felt hollow. And as he turned back to his work, hands steady but his thoughts anything but, he knew—he wasn't sure if that was a lie.

The Lighthouse Beanery, a small café on the corner of Shoreline Avenue, was precisely as Naomi remembered. The soft blue awning faded from sun and salt and fluttered slightly in the morning breeze. The door had the same brass bell that chimed gently when someone entered. Inside, the scent of freshly brewed espresso, warm pastries, and vanilla undertones wrapped around her like a familiar embrace. The place was cozy, with worn wooden tables, mismatched chairs, and shelves lined with books and succulents in tiny ceramic pots. Naomi sat at a corner table by the window, her fingers wrapped around a steaming mug of chamomile tea. She stared out at the ocean, waves rolling lazily onto the shore, their white crests catching the early afternoon light.

The view hadn't changed.

But she had.

Pain curled sharp and sudden in her abdomen, a fierce cramp that stole the air from her lungs like a thief in the night. She gritted her teeth, a sharp wince escaping her lips as she braced herself against the cool, worn surface of the table. Her fingers dug into the polished wood, the grain pressing into her skin as she fought to breathe through the wave of discomfort. For a fleeting moment, the intensity subsided, but the lingering ache didn't fully dissipate; it remained, a dull throbbing reminder that settled deep within, relentless and insistent, as if demanding her attention with every heartbeat.

"You're doing it again."

Naomi blinked and turned toward the voice. Willow Carmichael stood beside her table, arms crossed, eyebrows raised.

"Doing what?" Naomi asked, feigning innocence.

Willow slid into the seat across from her. "Pretending."

Naomi forced a smile. "I have no idea what you're talking about."

Willow wasn't buying it. She never did.

"You need to tell him," Willow said quietly.

Naomi's stomach twisted. She knew exactly who Willow meant.

"I don't need to tell anyone," she murmured.

Willow sighed. "He deserves to know."

Naomi shook her head. "He deserves someone who stays."

A silence stretched between them, filled only by the soft clinking of coffee cups and the low hum of conversation around them.

After a moment, Willow leaned forward. "And what about you?"

Naomi frowned. "What about me?"

"You deserve someone who stays, too."

Naomi swallowed hard, feeling the lump in her throat swell as she turned her gaze back to the window. The rain pattered softly against the glass, blurring the view of the world outside. She could see the faint outlines of trees swaying gently in the breeze, their leaves shimmering with droplets. Though the words never escaped her lips, they echoed in her mind with stubborn urgency: I don't have time to stay. A sense of fleeting urgency tugged at her, reminding her of the responsibilities waiting for her, the moments slipping away like the clouds overhead.

The afternoon sun hung low in the sky, casting golden streaks over the wooden planks of the boardwalk. The air smelled of salt, fried seafood, and melting ice cream, mingling with the distant sound of waves crashing against the shore. Naomi walked slowly, one hand tucked into the pocket of her light cardigan, her sandals clicking softly against the aged wood. And then—she collided with something solid—or rather, someone.

Strong, steady hands gripped her arms, anchoring her before she could stumble. As her breath hitched in her throat, she looked up to meet stormy blue eyes that seemed to hold a world of emotion—familiar, searching, unmistakable. Graham. For a fleeting moment, the air thickened, and she felt a suffocating rush as memories danced ominously in the space between them. She recalled the warmth of his arms enveloping her, the tender way he would tuck a rebellious strand of hair behind her ear, and the nights they spent intertwined, whispering promises that felt as endless as the stars. Yet now, an unbridgeable distance lay between them—time, pain, and unspoken hurt woven into the fabric of their past.

She stepped back. "Hi."

It was an awful greeting, hollow and inadequate. But it was all she had. His eyes swept over her, and she felt something shift, something fragile and uncertain.

"You okay?" he asked.

Too quick, too practiced, she smiled. "Yeah. Just... tired."

His brow furrowed. "You were always a bad liar."

Before she could respond, a voice interrupted them. "Graham?"

Naomi pivoted slightly, her breath catching in her throat as Hanna Richards gracefully approached, her golden hair glinting in the sunlight, vibrant green eyes darting curiously between them. A heavy recognition settled in Naomi's chest, cold and unyielding like a stone. It dawned on her that Graham hadn't been lingering in anticipation; he had moved on without her. Anger and hurt mingled in a tempest within her, causing her fingers to clench into tight fists. With effort, she forced a smile onto her lips, though it felt like a mask over her turmoil.

"I should go."

And this time, she didn't look back when she walked away.

Chapter Three: A Promise to Herself

The house was quiet. Naomi longed for quiet when she lived in the city when the world was too loud, fast, and demanding. She had spent years drowning in the chaos of deadlines, airports, and unfamiliar hotel rooms. Now, the silence pressed in around her like a weight. She sat cross-legged on her childhood bed, the floral quilt beneath her softened by time and a thousand washes. Her fingers traced the familiar fabric as she let her gaze drift across the room—old bookshelves lined with forgotten paperbacks, a bulletin board pinned with yellowed photographs, a row of sea glass jars on the windowsill, their colors dulled from years of dust.

Everything had stayed the same, only she had changed.

Naomi exhaled and shifted her focus to the leather-bound journal in her lap. The spine was cracked from years of use, and the pages were worn at the edges. Pressed wildflowers slipped out between them, and Polaroids of summers long past tumbled onto the mattress. She picked up one of the photos. A younger version of herself stood on the bow of a boat, arms outstretched, laughing, the wind teasing her dark waves loose from their braid. Graham had taken the picture, capturing the exact moment before she had turned to him and said, "I never want this day to end."

Naomi swallowed hard. She reached for a pen and flipped to a blank page, the ink bleeding deep into the paper as she wrote.

The List
☐ Watch a sunrise with someone I love.
☐ Dance barefoot in the rain.
☐ Leave a note in The Turning Page for someone to find.
☐ Eat a whole lemon cake from Ever After Bakery.
☐ Take a boat ride one last time.
☐ Write my final letters.
☐ Watch the last sunset.

Her fingers hovered hesitantly above the carefully inked words on the parchment, the weight of each letter heavy with unspoken truths. She hadn't penned the phrase, "Get better," because deep down, she understood that the reality of it was far more complicated than mere wishes or hopeful sentiments. The truth settled in her chest like a cold stone, sharp and immovable, casting a shadow over her heart that felt impossible to lift. She pressed her thumb firmly over the still-glossy ink, hoping against hope that by some miracle, she could seize these fleeting moments of clarity and emotion, freezing them in time so they would last forever, untouched by the relentless march of reality.

"I can do this," she whispered.

She closed the journal, pressing it to her chest as if holding it close would keep time from slipping through her fingers. But she already knew—time was not something she could have.

When Naomi entered The Turning Page, the scent of coffee and old books wrapped around her. The bookstore had always been a safe place. Even as a child, she had spent hours tucked into the corner reading nooks, running her hands over the spines of novels, wondering what stories they held. Now, the space was unchanged—dark wooden shelves stood tall along the walls, their surfaces lined with tiny ceramic pots of succulents. The cash register sat beneath the soft glow of an old Edison bulb, and the faint scent of vanilla candles lingered in the air.

Willow stood behind the polished wooden counter, her fingers absentmindedly adjusting her thick-rimmed glasses as she peered closely at the cluttered inventory sheets spread out before her. The aroma of freshly brewed coffee filled the air, and a steaming ceramic cup perched precariously at the edge of the counter, its warmth radiating toward her. She blinked away the exhaustion that clung to her like a shadow and looked up, her expression softening as she caught sight of the familiar faces of regular customers filtering into the quaint little shop. The morning sunlight streamed through the front window, casting gentle shadows that danced across the floor, creating a cozy ambiance that made the space feel like a warm embrace.

"You're up early."

Naomi smiled, slipping her hands into her cardigan pockets. "Couldn't sleep."

Willow didn't push. She watched as Naomi wandered toward the poetry section, her gaze thoughtful. Naomi ran her fingers along the spines, stopping when she reached a worn copy of Mary Oliver's poems. She flipped through it, found a blank space in the margins of one page, and carefully tucked a folded piece of paper inside. The note read: We never know how much time we have left. So, love fiercely, live boldly, and don't be afraid to be remembered. She closed the book and slid it back onto the shelf.

Behind her, Willow exhaled, shaking her head. "You never used to write things down like this."

Naomi hesitated. "I never used to count the days."

Silence.

Willow's jaw tightened. "Oh goodness, Naomi."

But she didn't stop her.

The docks smelled of salt and sun-warmed wood, the gentle lap of water against the pilings filling the air with a rhythmic hush. Seagulls circled overhead, their cries sharp against the morning sky. Naomi stood at the edge of the pier, her fingers curled around the railing, watching the boats bob gently in their slips. Her chest tightened. She hadn't been on a boat in years. She took a slow breath, stepping closer—

"You thinking about stealing one, or do you need a captain?"

Naomi was startled, her heart stuttering as she turned.

Graham.

He leaned against one of the weathered dock posts, arms crossed, casually surveying the bustling harbor. The late afternoon sun cast a warm glow on his thoughtfully worn faded navy T-shirt, which clung slightly to his frame, hinting at the day's labor. The salty breeze tousled his hair and brought the scent of the sea, mixing with the earthy aroma of freshly cut wood, creating a familiar backdrop to the serene chaos around him.

She swallowed. "Do you always sneak up on people?"

One side of his mouth twitched. "Only the ones who look like they're about to make bad decisions."

She rolled her eyes, but her lips smiled.

He stepped forward, nodding toward the water. "Want a ride?"

Naomi hesitated, her breath catching in her throat. The vivid memory of that old Polaroid flickered in her mind—she could almost feel the crisp autumn air against her skin, the gentle tug of the wind lifting her hair as she stood on the cliff's edge. Graham's laughter rang out, light and carefree, as she spread her arms wide, pretending to take flight, the sun casting a warm glow around them. The colors of the leaves were ablaze with shades of orange and gold, a perfect backdrop to their youthful exuberance.

Her fingers curled into her sweater sleeve. "I don't know."

Graham's expression softened.

"Come on, Andrews." He reached for the rope, untying the boat from the dock. "I won't let you drown."

Her breath hitched. It was such a simple sentence. But something about how he said it made her want to believe him. She stepped onto the boat.

The boat cut smoothly through the water, the low hum of the engine blending with the rush of waves. The sky stretched wide and open above them, the ocean endless in every direction. Naomi leaned against the railing, her wavy brown hair whipping in the wind and her chest expanding with the scent of salt, sun, and what felt like freedom. For the first time in a long time, she felt light. Graham closely watched her.

"You always loved being out here."

"Yeah. I always have."

But there was something in the way she said it, a tone that felt irrevocable as if sealing a door that could never be re-opened. His gaze lingered on her, tracing the curve of her downcast eyes, flickering with unshed tears. He noticed how she pressed a hand to her stomach, a subtle gesture that betrayed a hidden tension, a habit she seemingly assumed he wouldn't notice when her guard was down. Her breath caught—a soft, almost imperceptible hitch—too frequent, too raw as if each inhalation were a struggle. Something wasn't right. For the first time, the thought struck him like a slow-moving wave, an unsettling realization that washed over him, tugging at the edges of his consciousness and forcing him to confront the gravity of the moment.

They pulled back into the marina as the sun dipped lower in the sky, casting long shadows across the wooden planks. Naomi stepped onto the dock first, shaking off the boat's lingering sway. Graham leaned against a wooden post, arms crossed. He watched her carefully now, his storm-blue eyes unreadable.

"You're different."

She didn't answer.

Instead, she smiled. "Thanks for the boat ride, Captain."

Graham's lips twitched. "Anytime, Andrews."

But as she walked away, his brows furrowed, and for the first time, suspicion took root in his chest.

Chapter Four: The Cracks Deepen

The scent of fresh-cut cedar and varnish filled the air, the rhythmic scrape of sandpaper against wood usually grounding Graham. But today, he was off. His hands moved over the grain of an unfinished tabletop, the soft hiss of sanding filling the shop, but his focus had been fractured since the moment Naomi walked back into his life. She had unsettled something in him—something he wasn't ready to name. Outside, the golden light of late afternoon stretched across the bay, the docks swaying gently with the tide. But inside, the air felt heavy.

"You're distracted again," Beck's voice cut through the quiet.

Graham glanced up from his book, his brow furrowing slightly as he caught sight of his younger brother. Leaning casually against the doorframe, his arms crossed over a faded green t-shirt, the boy was a picture of relaxed confidence. Sunlight streamed in from behind him, casting a warm halo around his tousled hair, while a sly smirk danced on his lips, hinting at some private joke or mischief yet to be revealed. The faint sound of laughter from the living room added to the atmosphere, making the moment feel both lighthearted and teasingly charged.

"I'm working," Graham muttered.

"No, you're brooding."

Graham sighed, setting the sandpaper down. "You

need something, or you just here to bother me?"

Beck shrugged. "Bit of both." He walked over, inspecting the wood Graham had been sanding, before glancing back at his brother. "So, you gonna admit it?"

"Admit what?"

"That Naomi's been on your mind since the second she came back into town."

Graham's jaw tightened.

Beck chuckled. "I mean, come on, man. She leaves without a word, disappears for ten years, then suddenly reappears, looking like she's hiding something. And you're not the least bit curious?"

Graham hesitated. Then, in a voice that was too low, too careful, he said, "She's not just hiding something." He looked at Beck, his expression unreadable. "She's different."

Beck studied him for a long moment before nodding slowly. "You sure you wanna go looking for answers, though?" His tone shifted, losing its teasing edge. "Because if you start digging, you might not like what you find."

Graham didn't respond.

Because that was precisely what he was afraid of.

At the Andrews' home, the rich, inviting aroma of freshly brewed coffee mingled with the crisp, buttery scent of warm toast, creating a cozy atmosphere in the kitchen. Naomi sat at the sturdy oak table, her fingers delicately curled around a large, cerulean ceramic mug, the surface smooth and cool against her skin. The early morning sunlight streamed through the lace-trimmed curtains, casting intricate, golden patterns on the polished wooden floor, every dust mote dancing in the beams of light. Despite the warmth surrounding her, a restless unease settled in Naomi's chest, clouding her thoughts as she absentmindedly traced the rim of the mug, lost in a swirl of contemplation.

Across from her, her father, Thomas Andrews, sat with his salt and pepper hair neatly combed back, the strands catching the morning light that filtered through the window. A newspaper lay unfolded on the table in front of him, its pages slightly crinkled, reflecting countless mornings spent sipping coffee and reading the news. The rich aroma of freshly brewed coffee wafted through the air, steam curling upward from the mug beside him, creating a warm and inviting atmosphere. Unlike Ruth, who had a habit of filling the silence with an endless stream of questions—her curiosity boundless—Thomas embraced the quiet moments, allowing them to unfold naturally, as if the silence itself had stories to share.

"You don't have to pretend with me," Ruth had said earlier.

And now, Thomas was saying the same thing—just without words.

For a while, the only sounds that filled the small café were the occasional rustle of newspaper pages, each crisp turn breaking the silence, and the distant hum of the radio softly playing an old Sinatra song, the smooth croon wrapping around her like a familiar, warm blanket. Naomi tried to sip her rich, dark coffee, allowing the warmth to spread through her hands as if she wasn't completely exhausted, her eyelids heavy with weariness. The fatigue gnawed at her, a relentless companion that seemed to betray her a little more with each passing day, leaving her to wonder how much longer she could maintain this façade of composure amidst the mounting shadows of her fatigue.

But then, her father spoke.

"You were always bad at pretending, kiddo."

Naomi blinked, looking up. "Excuse me?"

Thomas carefully folded the crumpled paper along its creased edges and set it aside on the polished oak table, the faint scent of varnish lingering in the air. Finally, he met her gaze, his striking blue eyes reflecting a mixture of determination and concern. They were the same piercing eyes that had once scrutinized her as a child, that exacting gaze unwavering when she attempted —albeit poorly—to fabricate stories about sneaking out past curfew to meet friends. The memories of those moments hung between them, a silent reminder of trust and the complexities of their relationship.

"I know you, Naomi. You think if you don't say it out loud, I won't see it." He leaned back in his chair, taking a slow sip of coffee. "But I do."

Her breath caught in her throat, a thick lump that threatened to choke her. For a fleeting moment, she was overwhelmed by the urge to confess, to spill her heart open and admit the truth—Dad, I'm dying. But the words felt like molten lava on her tongue, too hot to release. Instead, she dropped her gaze, her fingers tightening around the warm ceramic of her cup as if its comforting weight could ground her in the moment. The steam rose in delicate swirls, but all she could focus on was the silence between them. Her father didn't press her to speak; he was a man accustomed to patience. Yet, the gravity of his next words hung heavily in the air, an unspoken tension that settled like a dense fog, wrapping around them both.

"You don't have to carry everything alone, you

know."

Naomi swallowed hard, forcing a smile. "I think I'll head into town for a bit." She pushed back her chair. "Maybe stop by The Turning Page."

Thomas didn't argue. He simply nodded once, his eyes narrowing as he watched her slender figure retreating down the dimly lit hallway. The faint click of her heels against the polished floor echoed in the stillness, each step resonating with an air of finality. A troubled expression crossed his face as he contemplated the weight of their conversation, the tension lingering in the air long after she had turned the corner and disappeared.

The rich, inviting scent of freshly brewed espresso mingled with the sweet aroma of caramelized sugar, enveloping The Lighthouse Beanery in a warm embrace. Soft lights overhead cast a gentle glow, illuminating the dark wood countertops and the eclectic collection of vintage coffee grinders displayed on the walls. The quiet hum of conversation created a comforting background symphony, punctuated occasionally by the sharp hiss of the steamer as baristas worked diligently behind the counter.

Graham had not intended to stop here; the restlessness that clenched at his stomach drove him into the café on impulse. He had been feeling irritable all morning, desperately needing a caffeine fix to soothe his frayed nerves. As he pushed open the heavy door, the bell overhead jingled softly, marking his entrance. To his surprise, he spotted Hanna perched on a high barstool at the counter, a steaming cup of coffee cradled in her hands. Her dark hair fell in soft waves around her shoulders, and she looked up at him with a small, knowing smile that sent a rush of warmth through him. There was a familiarity in her gaze that both comforted and unsettled him as if she could see right through the exterior he carefully maintained.

"You don't usually come here for coffee," she said.

Graham exhaled, rubbing a hand over the back of his neck. "Guess I needed a change."

Hanna didn't move as he stepped beside her, ordering black coffee. She studied him, like she could see right through him.

"You're distracted," she said finally.

Graham didn't look at her. "Just a long day."

Hanna tilted her head slightly. "You mean Naomi."

His shoulders tensed, and for a second, neither of them spoke.

Then, she smiled, but there was something sad about it. "She's always had that effect on you, hasn't she?"

Graham turned to her then, finally meeting her gaze. "It's not like that."

Hanna didn't argue. But she didn't agree, either.

The sky had begun to darken, soft shades of rose and amber bleeding into the horizon like watercolors on a canvas. The boardwalk stretched long and quiet, weathered planks beneath Naomi's feet creaking gently with each step. The distant sound of the tide rolling in and out provided a steady hum, the rhythmic crashing of waves against the shore resonating deep within her, a reminder of nature's constancy. She needed the ocean today, its vastness offering solace, a stark contrast to the chaos swirling in her mind. Here, she felt tethered to something real, something steadfast, when everything else felt like it was slipping away. Footsteps sounded behind her, echoing softly as they approached, but she kept her gaze fixed on the horizon.

"You always used to love sunsets."

Naomi's heart stilled. She turned, finding Graham standing there, hands in his pockets, watching her like he was trying to see beneath her skin.

"Still do," she murmured.

He stepped closer, falling into stride beside her. The air between them was heavy—not uncomfortable but charged.

"Why did you really come back?"

Naomi tensed.

"I told you," she said lightly. "I missed home."

Graham studied her, his expression unreadable. "That's not the whole story."

Naomi's fingers curled into her dress. "Some things aren't meant to be questioned, Graham."

"That's not an answer."

She met his gaze, her eyes reflecting an emotion that momentarily stole the breath from his lungs—a quiet kind of fear that shimmered like fragile glass, ready to shatter. In that fleeting instant, he sensed an unspoken farewell lingering in the depths of her gaze, heavy and poignant. The air between them crackled with unarticulated words, aching to break free. But just as he opened his mouth to bridge the chasm that had formed, she took a step back, her expression folding into a mask of resolve, leaving him grasping for what remained of their connection.

"Thanks for the walk," she whispered. Then she turned and disappeared down the beach.

And Graham stood there, staring after her, knowing—deep in his chest, deep in his bones—something was very, very wrong.

Chapter Five: The Truth Presses In

The kitchen smelled of coffee and the faintest trace of cinnamon, a comforting scent that had lingered in Naomi's childhood home for as long as she could remember. The sound of waves rolling in from the nearby shore filtered through the open window, their rhythmic crash a steady reminder that time moved forward, whether she was ready or not. Thomas Andrews sat at the head of the small wooden table, his large, calloused hands wrapped around a steaming mug of black coffee. He wasn't reading the newspaper like he usually did in the mornings. Instead, he was staring out the window, his gaze distant, his brow furrowed. Across the kitchen, Ruth moved in quiet, controlled motions, wiping down an already spotless countertop. She had always filled silence with movement, but today, the tension in the air was thick, pressing against them both.

She exhaled finally, setting the cloth aside. "She's getting worse."

Thomas didn't immediately look at her, but he nodded. "I know."

For weeks, they had circled the truth like wary animals, both acutely aware of the subtle yet profound changes unfolding in their daughter. Her laughter, once a bright melody that filled their home, had grown infrequent, overshadowed by a silence that weighed heavily in the air. They noticed how Naomi's once-vibrant spark in her eyes had dulled, replaced by a distant gaze that seemed to look beyond them, as if she were lost in a world of her own. Yet, they clung to the illusion that if they sidestepped the conversation—if they avoided naming the problem—it somehow wouldn't exist.

But now, the reality was undeniable. Naomi was slipping away from them, gradually retreating into a shadowy realm of confusion and despair that they could no longer ignore. Her room, once a vibrant sanctuary filled with laughter and creativity, now lay in disarray, the remnants of her beloved toys and art supplies gathering dust, reflecting the turmoil within her. Each passing day felt heavier, the weight of unspoken fears and unacknowledged pain pressing down on their hearts. As they stood together, staring at the daughter they once knew, a sense of urgency filled the air, urging them to confront the truth they had both been desperately trying to evade.

Ruth sat down across from her husband, her hands wringing together. "I keep telling myself if I don't push if I just give her space, she'll come to us when she's ready." Her voice wavered. "But what if she never does?"

Thomas leaned back in his chair, his expression unreadable. His wife had always been more vocal and outwardly emotional, but his love for Naomi ran just as deep. "We need to talk to her," he said, his voice steady. We need to make her listen."

Ruth hesitated, chewing on her bottom lip. "And if she refuses?"

Thomas' jaw tightened. "Then we don't give her the choice."

Both of them understood Naomi well—her unyielding stubbornness and her fierce independence that often set her apart from others. With every interaction, they had witnessed her relentless determination, the way she refused to back down even in the face of overwhelming odds. But this wasn't just about pride or her characteristic defiance. This was about the precious time they had left—a ticking clock that felt alarmingly loud in the silence between them. Each day seemed to slip away like sand through their fingers, leaving them anxious and aware of how little time was left to make meaningful choices and memories together.

The apartment was enveloped in a blanket of silence, the only sound punctuating the stillness was the soft ticking of the antique clock mounted on the wall, each tick resonating in the hushed space. Hanna sat on the edge of the bed, the plush comforter slightly rumpled beneath her. Her fingers instinctively gripped her phone, its screen glowing dimly in the soft light of the lamp beside her. She found herself staring intently at the message she had composed and sent an hour ago, her heart racing with anticipation and uncertainty. Shadows danced across the walls as the evening light faded, echoing her feelings of anxious hope and trepidation.

Can we talk?

Graham hadn't responded.

She swallowed hard, her throat dry as she gripped the phone tighter, fingers digging into smooth plastic. A month ago, she wouldn't have had to ask him for help; Graham would have already been there, just like always. She could almost picture him now, a warm smile on his face, arms wrapped securely around her waist, pressing a gentle kiss to her temple as he recounted the mundane details of his day at the shop—the sound of clinking tools, the scent of fresh paint mingling with coffee. But things had changed, and she felt that shift like a cold breeze sweeping through an open window, unsettling her. The connection they once shared was slipping away between them, like sand through her fingers, leaving her with nothing but empty memories. She knew why it was happening, the heavy weight of unspoken words hanging between them, suffocating the laughter and the easy rhythm they once had.

Naomi.

Hanna had never been naïve about Naomi's place in Graham's past. She had always known her fiancé had loved someone before her, and that love had left a mark. But Naomi had been gone for ten years, and Hanna had convinced herself that ghosts didn't return. Except they did. She let out a slow breath, closing her eyes for a brief moment before looking at her phone again.

No response.

She wasn't going to lose him. She refused to. The air inside the workshop smelled of sawdust and varnish, a thick and familiar scent. Late afternoon, light streamed through the open garage doors, casting long shadows across the workbenches. Beck was finishing a project, wiping down the surface of a newly sanded table, his hands coated in a fine layer of dust. He glanced up as Graham walked in, his brother's tension visible in how his shoulders squared.

"That's the same face you made when Mom caught us sneaking beers at seventeen," Beck said, smirking.

Graham ignored him, rubbing a hand over his face. "It's Naomi."

Beck's smirk faded. He set the cloth down and

leaned against the workbench, his expression shifting to something more serious. "Yeah?"

Graham exhaled sharply, his jaw tightening. "She's hiding something. I see it in how she moves and looks at me—" He broke off, shaking his head. "Something's wrong."

Beck studied him for a long moment before speaking. "And if you're right?"

Graham swallowed his throat tight. "Then I don't know what I'm supposed to do."

Beck didn't answer right away. Then, after a moment, he nodded. "Then maybe," he said carefully, "you should stop standing around and find out."

Naomi nestled into the worn, beige couch in the living room, her knees tucked beneath her as she gazed out the large bay window. The fading daylight painted the horizon in vibrant streaks of orange and soft pink, casting a warm glow over the room and highlighting the dust motes that danced lazily in the air. She could feel the weight of the moment settling in her chest; she had known this reckoning was approaching. The sound of footsteps echoed through the hallway, a slow, deliberate rhythm that sent a shiver of anticipation down her spine before she even turned to look.

"Sweetheart, we need to talk," Ruth said softly.

Naomi didn't turn immediately. She forced a small smile as she finally glanced over her shoulder. "That's never a good sign."

Her mother sat down beside her, her face lined with worry. Thomas remained standing, his presence steady, unmoving.

"We know, Naomi," Ruth murmured.

Naomi's breath caught. "Know what?"

Thomas' voice was quiet but firm. "That you're not okay."

The words hit her like a punch to the chest. She could lie. She could tell them she was tired and that they were worrying for no reason. But then she looked at her father—a man who had always been strong, steady, unshakable—and saw the concern in his eyes. And suddenly, the lie wouldn't come. The scent of salt and damp wood filled Naomi's lungs as she walked along the shoreline, the waves brushing gently against the sand. She needed to clear her head and breathe. She didn't hear the footsteps at first.

Then—"Tell me the truth."

She froze in place, her heart racing as time seemed to slow around her. Slowly, she turned to face him. Graham stood a few feet away, his hands casually tucked into the pockets of his worn jeans, but there was nothing casual about his demeanor. His expression, usually so easygoing, was now a mask of uncertainty, unreadable and intense. Yet it was his eyes—those stormy blue eyes—that captured her attention, swirling with a tempest of emotions, revealing something raw and unguarded, as if he held a secret on the brink of spilling over.

"Naomi," he said again, his voice lower now, rougher. She swallowed hard. "Graham…"

"Don't do that." He took a step closer, his jaw tightening. "Don't pretend everything's fine."

Her pulse pounded in her ears. "I don't know what you mean."

His hands curled into fists at his sides. "Dammit, Naomi, I see it. The way you move, the way you—" He let out a sharp breath. "You're sick, aren't you?"

The air between them stilled, heavy with unspoken

words and unfulfilled longing. Naomi's throat tightened, a knot of anxiety forming as the silence pressed in around them. For a fleeting moment, she contemplated lying, the prospect of telling him he was imagining things tempting her like a quick escape. But as she met his gaze, she encountered a vulnerability that shattered her resolve completely. His eyes, usually so vibrant, now held a storm of understanding that left her breathless. It was clear: he already knew the truth lurking beneath the surface, hidden by a fragile facade.

She opened her mouth to speak, desperate to articulate the whirlwind of emotions churning inside her. But no words came—only a bittersweet ache that echoed in the quiet space between them, a silent testament to everything that had been left unsaid.

Chapter Six: When the Walls Close In

The Blue Ember, a rooftop bar, was alive with the hum of conversation, soft jazz playing over the speakers, and the occasional clink of glasses filling the spaces between words. The scent of salt, citrus, and smoked vanilla bourbon hung in the warm air, blending with the low flicker of golden string lights that lined the railing. Hanna sat with her back to the ocean, facing Ezra Sinclair, who was watching her with careful scrutiny. The wine glass in her hand felt heavy, the chilled rosé untouched. Across from her, Ezra's old-fashioned rested half-finished, the ice melting in slow, lazy swirls.

"You're going to stare at your drink all night, or are we discussing the problem?" Ezra asked, raising an eyebrow as he leaned back in his chair. His fitted blazer stretched smoothly over his shoulders, his usual air of unshakable confidence somehow both reassuring and infuriating.

Hanna let out a slow breath, forcing herself to meet his gaze. "It's Graham."

Ezra's lips twitched, but his expression didn't shift. "Of course it is."

Hanna set the glass down, twisting the stem between her fingers. "He's pulling away." The words felt foreign, like saying them out loud made them real.

Ezra exhaled through his nose, swirling the amber liquid in his glass. "Because of Naomi."

Hanna flinched. There was no point in denying it. Ezra could read her better than anyone.

"She's in his head. She's always been in his head," Hanna admitted, voice barely above a whisper.

Ezra tilted his head, studying her. "Alright, let's get real—are we talking 'I'm slightly worried about my fiancé thinking about an ex' energy, or 'I'm watching my entire future slip through my fingers' energy?"

Hanna's stomach tightened. She knew the answer before she even spoke it.

"The second one."

Ezra didn't respond right away. He let the weight of her words settle between them, taking a slow sip of his drink before setting it down with a soft clink. His usual smirk was gone, replaced by something softer.

"Hanna," he said gently, "I need you to be real with yourself. Do you really think he's still yours?"

She swallowed hard, gripping the edge of the table. For the first time, she wasn't sure.

The house was quiet except for the distant sound of waves rolling onto shore.

Naomi sat curled in the oversized armchair near the window, her knees drawn up, fingers tracing the rim of her coffee mug. She had barely touched the drink, which was now lukewarm and forgotten. Across from her, Graham sat on the couch, elbows braced on his knees, hands clasped tightly. The dim light from the lamp on the side table cast deep shadows across his face, but she could still see the tension in his jaw, the way his knuckles had turned white.

"Naomi, don't lie to me."

His voice was quiet but firm, cutting through the thick silence between them.

She inhaled slowly, choosing her words carefully. "I'm not lying."

Graham shook his head, standing abruptly. "You are." He turned to face her, eyes burning with something raw. "I see it. You don't move the same. You barely eat. He exhaled sharply, raking a hand through his hair. "You're sick, aren't you?"

Naomi felt the weight of those words sink into her chest, pressing down, stealing the air from her lungs. She wanted to deny it, offer some excuse, and shift the conversation away from this unbearable truth. But she couldn't. Her throat tightened as she finally met his gaze. His stormy blue eyes searched hers, waiting, pleading for something she wasn't sure she had the strength to give.

"I don't have much time, Graham."

The confession left her lips in a whisper, barely more than a breath, but it shattered everything. Graham's face went slack, his expression crumbling into something unrecognizable. His lips parted slightly as if he would say something—but no words came. She saw the sheer devastation in his eyes for the first time.

And it broke her.

The Jameson & Co. Woodwork shop was silent, the usual comfort of sawdust and varnish offering no relief. The overhead lamp buzzed softly, casting a dim, golden glow over the workbench. Graham slammed the door shut behind him, bracing his hands against the table. His breath came in short, uneven bursts.

She's dying. The words replayed over and over in his mind like a cruel echo he couldn't escape. His hands curled into fists, his knuckles pressing into the wood, trying to ground himself in anything other than this unbearable truth.

"Good grief, man."

Graham turned at the sound of Beck's voice. His brother stood in the doorway, his brow furrowed in concern.

"What happened?" Beck asked, stepping closer.

Graham exhaled sharply, dragging a hand down his face. "It's Naomi."

Beck didn't say anything at first. He just watched, waiting, the way he always did when Graham was close to falling apart.

"Tell me," Beck said finally, his voice quieter now.

Graham let out a shaky breath. "She's sick." His throat tightened. "She's—"

The words wouldn't come. Beck's expression darkened, his jaw setting as he took another step forward.

"She's dying."

The admission felt like ripping open a wound he didn't know how to close.

Beck let out a slow breath, nodding once. "Alright."

Graham stared at him, anger bubbling beneath the surface. "Alright? That's all you have to say?"

Beck's expression didn't change. "No. But it's the only thing that makes sense right now."

Graham's fists clenched. He wanted to hit something, to punch through the unbearable weight pressing on his chest. Instead, he turned, gripping the edge of the workbench, trying to breathe. Beck stood beside him, silent, steady. He didn't offer empty words. Didn't tell him it would be okay. Because they both knew it wouldn't be.

Naomi sat alone in her childhood bedroom, staring

at the lamp's soft glow beside her. She thought about her parents—how her father's steady presence had cracked just enough to show his fear and how her mother's eyes had shimmered with unshed tears even as she tried to be strong. She thought about her friends—Graham, the weight of his devastation, the silent question in his gaze: Why didn't you tell me sooner? Hanna, who probably hated her. She thought about herself. And the life she wasn't ready to let go of.

She reached for her phone, her fingers trembling slightly as she scrolled through her contacts. Her doctor's number stared back at her.

Chapter Seven: The Weight of Truth

The morning light bled through the curtains, soft and golden, but Naomi felt nothing but the crushing weight of exhaustion. Her body had become foreign to her—a cage she no longer controlled, a vessel that failed her more each day. She lay still, curled on her side, pressing a hand against the curve of her swollen abdomen. The pressure was worse today. The tightness had spread into her ribs, making her breathing feel shallow and delicate. A deep inhale sent sharp pain across her stomach, radiating down her back, making her limbs feel heavy and weak. She swallowed, wincing at the familiar burn of nausea at the back of her throat. She was running out of time. A knock sounded at the door, gentle but startling enough to make her flinch.

"Naomi?"

Her mother's voice was careful, hesitant. She already knew Naomi was struggling but was giving her the choice to admit it.

Naomi closed her eyes briefly, then forced herself upright, clutching the mattress for balance as dizziness swam through her vision. The act of simply sitting up drained her.

"I'm awake," she called, though her voice sounded thinner than she'd meant.

A pause. Then— "Come downstairs, sweetheart. You need to eat."

Naomi didn't have the energy to argue.

The kitchen smelled like fresh coffee, toast, and something sweet, maybe fruit. Naomi's stomach recoiled before she even made it to the table. Her mother, Ruth, stood at the counter, arranging a small plate. She glanced over her shoulder when Naomi entered, eyes scanning her carefully. Naomi could tell Ruth was looking for something—changes in her daughter's face, the subtle clues she wasn't okay.

"Sit," Ruth said, setting the plate down at Naomi's usual spot. Scrambled eggs. Whole wheat toast. Sliced peaches.

Naomi hesitated before lowering herself onto the chair. The effort felt monumental. She gripped the edge of the table as the nausea surged again. The food in front of her looked harmless, but the thought of swallowing anything sent panic rising in her throat. Ruth sat across from her, her coffee cup cradled in both hands. She didn't push, didn't speak. Just waited. Naomi forced herself to pick up the fork, pressing a bite of eggs onto it. She lifted it to her lips, but the moment the food touched her tongue, her stomach twisted violently. She barely had time to shove back from the table before she bolted for the trash can. Her body rejected the food in harsh, shuddering waves. She felt her mother's hand rubbing slow, soothing circles on her back.

"Oh, sweetheart," Ruth whispered. Her voice was heartbreak-wrapped in softness.

Naomi squeezed her eyes shut, her throat raw. She felt Ruth's hands tighten around her shoulders as if she were trying to hold her together. Naomi turned slowly, breathless, her mother's eyes shining with unshed tears.

"I can't do this anymore," Ruth whispered. "You need to see a doctor."

She had promised herself she wouldn't go back to the doctor. She had spent weeks, months, avoiding sterile white walls and pitying eyes. The doctors had already told her there was no miracle waiting for her, no sudden reprieve from the inevitable.

She had accepted it. Hadn't she? But now, sitting in the passenger seat of her mother's car, she felt the tight coil of fear twisting low in her stomach. The sign outside the office was clean and polished.

Dr. Madeline Hartwell – Oncology. A new doctor. A fresh pair of eyes. It shouldn't matter. But it did. She barely remembered stepping inside. The waiting room was quiet, and the walls were painted a calming shade of blue. A small water fountain trickled softly in the corner. It smelled like antiseptic and something floral. She sat stiffly in the chair, her hands curled into fists in her lap. Ruth filled out the paperwork, stealing glances at Naomi every few moments as if expecting her to change her mind and walk out. Maybe she should. Maybe she should pretend she never came.

But then—a name was called.

"Naomi Andrews?"

The weight in her chest felt like a leaden anchor as she rose to her feet, the cool, sterile air of the hospital corridor wrapping around her like a shroud. This was it—no turning back now. With a deep breath to steady her racing heart, she abandoned the facade she had clung to for far too long. There was no more room for denial. She followed the nurse down the dimly lit hallway, each step echoing in the stillness—a silent admission that she wasn't ready to let go, not yet. The walls seemed to close in, but with every determined footfall, she found a flicker of resolve igniting within her.

At the shore, Graham sat in his truck, his hands gripping the steering wheel so tightly his knuckles had gone white. Naomi was dying. He couldn't wrap his mind around it, couldn't make sense of the rage, the fear, the grief that had lodged itself inside his chest like a bullet he couldn't remove. He had spent ten years learning how to live without her, and now... now she would be gone forever. A sharp knock on the passenger window made him jump.

Beck.

His brother didn't wait for an invitation before yanking the door open and sliding into the seat beside him.

"Mom said you left the shop early," Beck said, propping one arm against the door. "Figured I'd find you here."

Graham exhaled sharply, pressing the heels of his hands against his eyes.

"She told me." His voice sounded wrecked. "She told me she's dying."

Beck didn't speak right away.

Then— "Okay."

Graham let out a bitter laugh, dropping his hands. "Okay?"

Beck shrugged, his face unreadable. "What else am I supposed to say?"

"I don't know," Graham snapped. "Tell me it's not real. Tell me there's some way to fix this."

Beck's jaw tightened. "There's not."

Graham let out a shuddering breath. He knew that.

Beck leaned forward, resting his arms on his knees. "So, what are you going to do?"

Graham blinked. "What?"

Beck turned to him, his expression steady, unreadable. "You're sitting here like you've already lost her. But she's still here, man."

Graham swallowed hard, looking away.

Beck's voice softened. "Maybe instead of wasting time being angry at the universe, you should figure out how you want to spend whatever time she's got left."

The words settled in Graham's chest like weight because Beck was right.

She was still here. And he wasn't going to waste another second.

Chapter Eight: The Unavoidable Truth

Dr. Madeline Hartwell's office walls were painted in soft gray, likely meant to be calming, but to Naomi, they only made the space feel colder. The air smelled of disinfectant, and the faint hum of a computer filled the silence. Across the desk, Dr. Hartwell scrolled through Naomi's records, her expression composed but not unfeeling. Naomi sat still, her hands folded in her lap. She had been through this before, staring at medical scans and waiting for a doctor to confirm what she already knew. But this time, it was different. This was the last time.

Dr. Hartwell turned the screen toward her. "I won't sugarcoat this, Naomi. The scans show continued progression."

Naomi's gaze flickered to the grayscale images of her body. The words beside them blurred together, but she could still make out the ones that mattered.

Stage IV Ovarian Cancer – Progression Noted.
Ascites Worsening – Severe Fluid Retention Present.
Increased Malnutrition & Muscle Wasting.
Metastasis to Surrounding Organs – No Curative Treatment Available.

She exhaled slowly, keeping her expression blank. She had known, of course. But seeing it laid out so plainly stole something from her.

Her mother, Ruth, sat beside her, silent and stiff. Her hands were clasped tightly in her lap, her knuckles white. Naomi could feel the tension radiating off her, but she didn't look at her. She couldn't.

"How much time?" Naomi asked, her voice steady.

Dr. Hartwell hesitated. "It's difficult to say. If we focus on symptom management, we might be looking at months. It depends on how well your body tolerates the medications. Months. Not years. Not even one full year."

The end was coming faster than she had hoped.

Dr. Hartwell leaned forward slightly. "Naomi, if there's anything else—any last tests or clinical trials you want to consider—this would be the time to ask."

Naomi shook her head. "No. Just the medications."

She was tired of hoping for miracles.

Dr. Hartwell nodded. "We'll focus on keeping you comfortable."

She went through the prescriptions—pain management, nausea relief, anxiety control, and fluid retention medication. The words blurred together, each one a reminder that she was no longer fighting for her life, just making the descent a little easier.

Graham sat at the edge of the worn, beige couch, its fabric frayed from years of use, his hands clasped tightly between his knees. Sunlight streamed through the half-drawn curtains, casting a warm glow but failing to alleviate the chill creeping into his chest. He had rehearsed this conversation a dozen times in front of the bathroom mirror, each time refining his words until they felt just right. Yet now, in the apartment that held the weight of countless memories—echoes of laughter, whispered secrets, and lingering shadows of bygone comfort—every word felt painfully inadequate. The air was thick with unspoken tensions, and the familiar scent of old books and brewing coffee suddenly felt suffocating, leaving him grappling with the heavy silence that hung between them.

Hanna stood near the tall, frost-laden window, her arms wrapped tightly around herself as if trying to ward off more than just the chill of the winter air. The soft, muted light from the overcast sky poured through the glass, casting a gentle glow on her features. She gazed at the snowflakes swirling outside, lost in her thoughts, not yet ready to meet his eyes. The tension in the room was palpable, thickening the air between them, as moments stretched into silence.

"You're pulling away," she finally said, her voice quiet but certain.

Graham exhaled, rubbing a hand over his face. "I don't know how to do this, Hanna."

She let out a bitter laugh, shaking her head. "Do what? Pretend like you're not still in love with her?"

His stomach twisted. "It's not—"

"Don't lie to me, Graham."

The words cut through him, sharp and final. Silence stretched between them, thick and unbearable.

Hanna swallowed hard, her voice raw. "You love her, don't you?"

Graham clenched his jaw tightly, the muscles in his face taut with frustration. He hadn't meant for this to happen, not after all the effort he had put in to reclaim his life. Morning after morning, he had forced himself to rise, to engage with the world around him, to build a semblance of a new life without Naomi. He had thrown himself into work, immersed himself in projects that once sparked his passion, and surrounded himself with friends who offered distraction. But the truth was undeniable now, sinking into his chest like a lead weight. No matter how hard he tried to forget the sound of her laughter or the way her eyes sparkled when she was excited, the memories lingered, clawing their way back to the surface.

He closed his eyes for a moment before looking at her. "Yes."

A breath shuddered from Hanna's lips. She nodded once, slowly, as if she had known the answer all along but had been waiting to hear it out loud.

"I don't hate her," she whispered, almost to herself.

Graham frowned.

Hanna inhaled sharply, wiping at her face. "I hate this. I hate losing you to her, but I hate even more that she's losing everything."

His chest ached, not just for Naomi but for Hanna too, for what he was taking from her, even if he didn't mean to.

"I never wanted to hurt you," he said quietly.

She gave him a sad smile. "But you have."

She didn't ask him to stay. And he didn't ask for forgiveness.

Hanna knocked twice on the wooden door before pushing it open, just as she had done a hundred times before. The moment she stepped inside Ezra's apartment, she was enveloped by the warm, inviting scent of sandalwood and the rich aroma of leather that lingered in the air. The soft glow of the dimly lit room revealed Ezra sprawled across his well-worn couch, his casual attire—faded jeans and a loose white t-shirt—suggesting a lazy evening at home. A glass of deep red wine teetered dangerously on his knee, catching the light and casting a ruby hue across the tabletop cluttered with books and half-finished sketches. As she entered, Hanna couldn't help but smile at the familiar scene, feeling a deep sense of comfort wash over her.

He barely glanced up before speaking. "Tell me you didn't get dumped in my doorway."

Hanna exhaled sharply, kicking off her heels. "Not in the doorway. In my apartment, like a respectable woman."

Ezra sighed dramatically, setting his glass down. "Brutal."

She sank onto the couch beside him, pressing her face against his shoulder. "I don't know what to do with myself."

Ezra wrapped an arm around her, pulling her close. "Well, first, you're going to cry. Loudly. Ugly. And I'll pretend I don't notice the snot on my sleeve."

A weak laugh escaped her, a fleeting sound that hung awkwardly in the air, but it was short-lived. The corners of her mouth twitched for a moment before the weight of her emotions closed in on her once more. Tears burned at the edges of her vision, threatening to spill over like a dam ready to break. She pressed a trembling hand against her face, feeling the warmth of her skin contrasted by the chill of despair, desperately trying to hold them in. Each breath came in shaky gasps, as the anguish within her swelled, fighting to be released.

Ezra sighed, rubbing her back. "You knew this was coming, babe."

She swallowed hard. "That doesn't make it hurt any less."

Ezra didn't argue; instead, he wrapped his arms

around her, pulling her closer as if trying to shield her from the world outside. The warmth of his embrace enveloped them both, and he rested his chin lightly on the top of her head, feeling the tension in her shoulders slowly begin to ease. The gentle rhythm of their breathing filled the silence, creating a moment of connection that spoke louder than words ever could.

In her dreams, Naomi wasn't dying. She stood on the shore, the ocean stretching endlessly before her, golden light spilling across the water. The air smelled of salt and warmth, something familiar, something safe. Then, arms wrapped around her from behind. She didn't have to turn to know who it was.

"I've got you," Graham murmured, his breath warm against her ear.

She closed her eyes, leaning into him. "I don't want to leave."

His arms tightened around her. "Then don't."

She turned in his hold, looking up at him. His blue eyes were endless, filled with something profound, something unspoken. He cupped her face gently, his thumb brushing over her cheek.

"I love you, Naomi," he said softly.

She woke up crying. The sheets beneath her were damp, and her body curled into itself. The dream had felt too real, too vivid. And for the first time in a long time, she wished she hadn't woken up at all.

Chapter Nine: Embracing the Inevitable

In the quiet sanctuary of their home, the warm glow of a softly flickering lamp illuminated the faces of Ruth and Naomi, casting gentle shadows that danced along the walls. Ruth sat by Naomi's side, her heart heavy yet resolute, feeling the weight of sorrow mingled with love. Dr. Madeline Hartwell had delivered the news with tender compassion, her voice calm but firm, conveying that the time had come to shift their focus from aggressive curative treatment to a path of comfort and peace. The word "hospice," laced with finality and grace, hung in the air like a fragile butterfly, a bittersweet acknowledgment of the inevitable journey's end approaching. Ruth glanced at Naomi, whose once-vibrant eyes now held a softness reflective of acceptance, and the room was filled with a poignant silence that spoke of shared memories and unspoken words.

"Mom," Naomi's voice was soft but steady, "I want to spend my remaining time here with you, surrounded by the things I love."

Ruth nodded, tears brimming but unshed. "We'll make sure of it, sweetheart. Every moment will be filled with love."

Together, they meticulously coordinated with the hospice team, transforming their home into a serene haven of peace. A hospital bed, dressed in soft, light-blue linens, was carefully positioned by the garden window, providing Naomi with a perfect view of the vibrant blooming flowers she had lovingly nurtured over the seasons. The sweet, calming scent of lavender, courtesy of the freshly cut sprigs arranged on her bedside table, wafted gently through the room, mingling seamlessly with the soft melodies of her favorite songs that softly played from a nearby speaker. The combination of sights and sounds created an atmosphere of tranquility, allowing Naomi to find comfort in her cherished memories as she gazed out at the garden she adored.

The afternoon sun streamed through the window, casting a golden glow illuminating Naomi's room, filling it with soft warmth. Willow stepped inside, her heart fluttering with excitement as she held a scrapbook in her hands, its cover decorated with vibrant ribbons in shades of turquoise and coral. The pages peeked out, hinting at the treasure trove of memories. When their eyes met, a silent understanding passed between them, a mix of anticipation and nostalgia that spoke volumes without a single word. The air was thick with the scent of blooming jasmine from the garden outside, creating an inviting atmosphere for their shared moments to unfold.

"I brought this," Willow said, settling beside Naomi, "thought we could reminisce a bit."

Naomi smiled, her fingers tracing the scrapbook's cover. "Remember our trip to the beach? We got so sunburned."

Willow laughed softly. "And we swore we'd never tell our moms."

As they turned the pages of the worn scrapbook, vibrant images of their adventures sprang to life—

camping under the vast expanse of starry skies, where the Milky Way twinkled like a million diamonds above them; impromptu road trips with windows rolled down, the wind tousling their hair as they sang along to their favorite songs, and countless moments of shared joy captured in photographs—faces aglow with laughter around a crackling campfire, and sandy smiles at the beach where they had built castles and splashed in the waves. The sound of their shared laughter gradually faded into a comfortable silence, each lost in a treasure trove of cherished memories, their hearts warmed by the bonds they had formed and the adventures yet to come.

"Willow," Naomi's voice broke the quiet, "there's something I regret."

Willow squeezed her hand gently. "Graham?"

A tear slipped down Naomi's cheek. "I never told him how much he meant to me."

Willow nodded, her own eyes glistening. "It's not too late, you know."

In the dim light of his study, Thomas stared at the photograph of a young Naomi on his desk. His little girl was now facing a battle he couldn't fight for her.

He clenched his fists, anger, and helplessness warring within him. The weight of impending loss pressed down, threatening to crush him.

A soft knock interrupted his turmoil. Ruth stood at the door, her eyes mirroring his pain.

"She needs us," she whispered.

Thomas took a shuddering breath, nodding. "I don't know how to say goodbye."

Ruth crossed the room, wrapping her arms around him. "Then let's not. Let's make every moment count."

Thomas found himself weighed down by an

overwhelming sense of helplessness and sorrow as he reflected on cherished memories with his daughter, whose health was rapidly declining. Late nights were spent sifting through photo albums, remembering her laughter during family vacations and how her eyes sparkled with determination. Faced with the impending loss, he recognized the importance of seeking support, so he contacted local support groups and professional counselors. Each session became a refuge where he could freely express his deepest fears and vulnerabilities. Gradually, he found solace in the shared experiences of others who understood the pain of impending separation, allowing him to feel less isolated in his grief and more connected to a community that offered empathy and understanding.

Across town, Hanna and Ezra sat in their bustling office, reviewing the latest request from a new client. Sterling & Stone Legal Partners, a prestigious law firm, had recently won a landmark case and desired a celebration to match their success.

"They want grandeur," Ezra mused, scanning the brief.

Hanna nodded thoughtfully. "A night to remember. Let's give it to them."

Their dedication to crafting unforgettable experiences shone through as they brainstormed themes and venues. Little did they know how their paths would soon intertwine with Naomi's journey.

Hanna and Ezra, a dynamic duo of event planners renowned for their innovative approach and attention to detail, were approached by Sterling & Stone Legal Partners, a prestigious law firm celebrated for their recent high-profile case victory involving a landmark decision that garnered national attention. Eager to celebrate this remarkable achievement, the firm sought to host an extravagant celebration that would commemorate its success and elevate its reputation within the legal community and beyond. Tasked with this significant endeavor, Hanna and Ezra were determined to organize an event that reflected the firm's status, combining elegance, sophistication, and a touch of grandeur to leave a lasting impression on their guests.

The ocean's rhythmic waves mirrored the turmoil in Graham's heart as he walked along the shore. Memories of Naomi flooded his mind—their shared dreams, stolen kisses, and the unspoken words that now weighed heavily on his soul. He had let her slip away, pride and fear holding him back. But the news of her illness shattered those barriers, leaving only the raw truth of his enduring love. Determined, he turned away from the sea, a newfound resolve guiding his steps. He would not let regret be their final chapter. Heart pounding, Graham stood at Naomi's doorstep, the weight of unspoken feelings pressing down on him. Ruth opened the door, surprise flickering across her face before she stepped aside, allowing him entry. He found Naomi in her room, the soft hum of her favorite song playing in the background. Her eyes widened in surprise, then softened with unspoken emotion.

"Graham," she breathed, a smile tugging at her lips.

He crossed the room in two strides, taking her hand in his. "Naomi, I've been a fool. I let you go once, but I can't do it again. I love you.

Chapter Ten: Holding On, Letting Go

The weight of fatigue pressing heavily on her limbs made sitting up feel like a Herculean task. Sunlight streamed through the sheer curtains, draping her pale skin in a warm golden glow and illuminating the quiet sanctuary of her small space. A cup of tea, still steaming, rested on the nightstand, a thoughtful gesture from Ruth that conveyed comfort even in her waking state.

Today, the pain was a manageable whisper rather than a shout. The medications worked their magic, cocooning her in a fragile sense of comfort. There was no crushing tightness in her chest, no piercing twinges to wrestle with—only that relentless fatigue, deep and pervasive, as if it were woven into the fabric of her bones, anchoring her to the bed with an unyielding weight. She turned her head slightly and saw Ruth sitting nearby, her face unreadable as she flipped through a book. It was a comfort to have her mother close, knowing she didn't have to fight this alone.

"Good morning," Naomi whispered, her voice raspy.

Ruth's head snapped up immediately, her lips curving into a soft smile. "Good morning, sweetheart. How are you feeling?"

"Tired." Naomi shifted slightly, trying to find a more comfortable position. "But okay."

Ruth reached over, brushing a strand of hair away from Naomi's face. "The nurse is coming by in a little while. She said your fluid buildup isn't worsening."

"That's good," Naomi murmured, though she didn't feel much relief. Good meant temporary.

A silence stretched between them before Ruth spoke again, her voice hesitant. "You up for a little distraction? I found some old photos yesterday."

Naomi nodded, and Ruth reached for a small box on the nightstand. Inside were scattered memories—polaroids, printed pictures from the early 2000s, even some old love notes Naomi had written in her teenage years. Naomi picked up a photo of her and Graham from years ago. They were young, carefree, and glowing with the kind of love that felt unbreakable at the time. Her fingers traced over Graham's face, her chest tightening with unspoken words.

Ruth watched her carefully. "You should tell him, you know."

Naomi sighed, placing the photo back in the box. "I think he already knows."

Hanna stared at her phone, her fingers hovering over the keyboard for too long. It felt wrong, texting him now, offering something when she wasn't sure she had a place in his life anymore. But she couldn't ignore the gnawing feeling in her chest—the need to help in some way, to be helpful when everything felt so out of her control.

Finally, she typed out a simple message: *Hey, I know things are hard right now. If there's anything I can do, just let me know.*

She hit send before she could second-guess herself, then immediately regretted it. Minutes passed, and then her phone vibrated.

Graham: *I appreciate it, Hanna, but I've handled it. Thank you, though.*

She exhaled slowly, staring at the response as a dull ache settled in her chest. He was kind, but distant. She had expected it, but it still hurt. Foolish. That's what she felt like. Foolish for thinking there was still something between them.

When he let her inside, Hanna knocked on Ezra's apartment door an hour later, not bothering with pleasantries. "Tell me I'm an idiot."

Ezra raised an eyebrow, flopping onto his couch. "I mean, I wasn't going to say it out loud, but since you asked..."

She groaned, dropping onto the chair opposite him. "I texted Graham. Asked if there was anything I could do to help."

Ezra made a face. "And?"

"He thanked me and declined." She shook her head. "I don't know what I was expecting."

Ezra leaned forward, resting his elbows on his knees. "Be honest with me—do you want to help him, or are you hoping he'll turn around and realize he's still in love with you?"

Hanna looked away, guilt creeping up her spine. "I don't know."

Ezra sighed, shaking his head. "Hanna, you need to stop waiting for him. He's not a project. He's not some puzzle you must piece back together after Naomi is gone."

She flinched at the bluntness of his words.

"You're an amazing person," Ezra continued, his voice softer. "But you can't live your life in limbo, waiting for Graham to pick you. He's a grown man. He will figure things out on his own."

She nodded, though it hurt.

Ezra leaned back with a smirk. "Besides, you're way too hot to waste your time on a guy who doesn't see it."

She laughed despite herself. "Thanks, Ezra."

Ruth was in the kitchen when she heard the sound—sharp, gasping breaths. She turned quickly, her eyes landing on Thomas, who was gripping the counter with white-knuckled hands. His face was pale, and his chest rose and fell far too fast.

"Thomas?" Her voice was laced with panic as she moved toward him.

"I—" He clenched his jaw, his breaths coming in shallow bursts. "I can't—breathe."

Her heart lurched. "Sit down. Now."

He sank into a chair, his hand pressed to his chest, his entire body trembling.

Ruth grabbed her phone, dialing 911 as fear clawed at her throat. "I think my husband is having a heart attack," she told the dispatcher.

Within minutes, the sirens wailed in the distance, growing louder as the paramedics arrived. Clad in their navy uniforms, they moved swiftly and efficiently, assessing the man lying on the ground. One medic knelt beside him, checking his pulse and looking for signs of injury, while another unpacked medical supplies from their kit, ready to provide any necessary treatment. The air was tense and urgent as the paramedics communicated quickly. Each movement was deliberate and practiced, and all were aimed at ensuring the man's safety and well-being.

Naomi, who had heard the commotion, tried to get up. "I need to go with him."

One of the paramedics shook his head. "We'll call you as soon as we know more."

Ruth turned to Naomi, her expression torn. "Stay here, sweetheart."

And then, just like shadows fading at dusk, they were gone, leaving an eerie silence that whispered their absence. The vibrant laughter that had filled the air moments before vanished, replaced by a stillness that hung like a heavy curtain. The sun dipped below the horizon, casting long shadows across the space where they had stood as if the world held its breath in disbelief at their sudden departure.

Naomi sat in silence, her hands gripping the frayed edges of the blanket that lay across her lap, its familiar fabric offering little comfort. The flickering light of the candle on the table cast dancing shadows on the walls, creating an unsettling atmosphere. For the first time in this relentless battle, a heavy realization settled over her: she wasn't simply leaving behind the people who loved her—she was shattering their lives, like fragile glass shattered against the cold floor. Memories of laughter shared and moments cherished rushed through her mind, each one a reminder of the heartache her departure would cause. The weight of her decision pressed down on her chest, tightening her breath as she grappled with the enormity of the choice she faced.

The smell of oil and rubber filled the air as Graham and his brother, Beck, worked side by side at the wood shop.

Beck wiped the sweat from his forehead. "You're quiet today."

Graham shrugged. "A lot on my mind."

Beck leaned against the workbench. "Thinking about Naomi?"

Graham exhaled, nodding.

Beck grabbed a wrench, spinning it between his fingers. "You remember when Dad tried to fix the old truck himself instead of taking it to the shop?"

Graham smirked. "And he made it worse?"

Beck chuckled. "He was too stubborn. He swore he knew what he was doing."

Graham let out a breath. "He never admitted when he was wrong."

Beck nudged him. "Unlike you, who's finally learning?"

Graham gave him a look, but there was warmth behind it.

Beck sobered. "Life's short, man. You don't get a lot of do-overs. Say what you need to say before it's too late."

Graham nodded, the words sinking in.

Chapter Eleven: The Fragility of Time

The steady beeping of the heart monitor filled the sterile air of the hospital room, underscoring the uneasy silence that hung in the atmosphere. Thomas lay on the narrow hospital bed, his breathing gradually becoming steadier, though a lingering tightness gripped his chest like an iron vice. The panic attack had felt as if someone had knocked the wind out of him—quite literally—but thankfully, the rhythmic pulse of his heart remained strong and resolute.

Beside him, Ruth sat in a plush chair that seemed to swallow her whole, her fingers gently intertwined with his. She traced small circles over his knuckles with a soothing touch, her eyes filled with concern yet softened by a flicker of hope. The smell of antiseptic mixed with the faint scent of lavender from the diffuser in the corner, an attempt to create a more comforting environment amidst the clinical surroundings. Each breath Thomas took was an effort, yet with Ruth's presence grounding him, he felt a glimmer of reassurance amid the chaos of his emotions.

"You gave me a scare," she murmured.

Thomas let out a slow breath. "I scared myself."

A nurse with light brown hair in her twenties checked his vitals and marked notes on a clipboard.

"Your blood pressure is still high, Mr. Andrews, but it's stabilizing."

Dr. Martin, a middle-aged man with black hair, followed moments later, reviewing the EKG printout. "It wasn't a heart attack, but you had a severe panic episode. Your body is under extreme stress. If you don't manage it, you could put yourself at real risk for heart issues."

Thomas sighed. "I don't know how to manage this. I don't know how to—accept what's happening."

Dr. Martin studied him briefly before saying, "I will give you something to help calm your system down. A mild sedative now, and I'll prescribe twenty anti anxiety pills for when you need them."

Thomas didn't argue. He knew he needed it.

Minutes later, the nurse returned with the small vial of medication, her demeanor calm and reassuring. She expertly prepared the IV line, inserted the needle with practiced ease, and connected the medication. A warm wave of relief washed over him almost immediately, as the weight in his chest began to dissolve. It felt like a heavy stone had been lifted, allowing his anxious heart to settle into a more regular rhythm. Although his body still throbbed with the residual ache of panic and fear, the suffocating sensation that had made it feel like his heart was trying to escape the confines of his ribs had finally subsided, leaving him feeling a fragile sense of calm in its wake.

Once alone, Ruth sighed, resting her forehead against his arm. "Thomas, you have to take care of yourself. You can't fall apart."

His throat tightened. "She's our little girl, Ruth. And I can't save her."

Ruth squeezed his hand. "I know. But we can give

her something else."

Thomas turned to her, his eyes lined with exhaustion. "What?"

Ruth exhaled softly. "We can give her the best last summer of her life."

Silence stretched between them, the weight of her words settling in.

Finally, Thomas nodded. "Then that's what we'll do."

The morning sun had barely crept through the windows when Willow sat on the edge of Naomi's bed, already dressed in jeans and a fitted black top, her suitcase resting by the door.

"You're leaving," Naomi murmured.

Willow sighed, brushing her fingers through Naomi's hair. "Yeah. I have to get back to work. But you know I'll be back the second you need me."

Naomi swallowed the lump in her throat. "I hate this."

"I know." Willow squeezed her hand. "But I'm only a phone call away. And you have Graham. Your parents. You're not alone."

Naomi bit her lip, nodding.

"You're strong," Willow whispered. "And you're still here. So, make it count, okay?"

Naomi exhaled slowly. "I will."

Willow gently pressed her lips to her forehead, a tender farewell for the moment, then reached for the worn leather suitcase resting by the door. She entered the crisp evening air with a final, lingering glance back at the room filled with memories. The door clicked softly shut behind her, sealing the space in silence. And just like that, she was gone, leaving only the faint scent of her floral perfume lingering in the air.

The sawdust-laden air of Jameson & Co. Woodworks enveloped Graham like a well-worn quilt—familiar and comforting—but today, it carried a distinctly unsettling weight that he couldn't shake off. Rays of afternoon sunlight streamed through the grime-coated windows, casting a warm, golden hue over the worn wooden floor, where countless projects had left their mark in the form of deep, etched grooves. The rhythmic hum of saws in the background, which typically provided him with a sense of solace as he lost himself in the precision of his craft, now only amplified his disquiet and made his heart race. He could hear the sharp screech of blades against the wood and the faint thud of heavy logs hitting the ground, creating a symphony he had once found soothing but now felt was underscored with an ominous tension. Graham's eyes flicked around the workshop, noting the dust motes dancing through the shafts of light, each one seemingly a reminder of the unsettling thoughts clouding his mind.

Graham wiped his hands on his well-worn jeans, the fabric stiff with years of sawdust and resin, as he stared at the blueprint sprawled out before him on the workbench. The detailed drawings of a custom oak table, with its elegant curves and precise measurements, usually sparked his creativity, but his mind felt like a foggy forest, shrouded and impenetrable. He couldn't shake the image of Naomi from his thoughts—the way her laughter danced through the air or her eyes sparkled with a mix of mischief and warmth. All he could think of was her, and no amount of intricate designs or wood grain patterns could pull him back to the task at hand.

Beck leaned against the workbench, watching him.

"You look like a guy about to say something important."

Graham sighed. "I need to cut back my hours."

Beck didn't look surprised. "For Naomi?"

"Yeah." Graham exhaled. "She doesn't have much time left. I don't want to waste a second of it."

Beck nodded. "Then don't. We'll hire someone new. I already have a few guys in mind."

Graham glanced at him. "You're okay with this?"

Beck smirked. "You're my brother, Graham. And you love her. Go be with her."

For the first time in days, Graham felt a flicker of certainty about the path he had chosen. The weight of indecision that had plagued him for so long began to lift, replaced by a cautious hope.

That night, Naomi lay propped up in bed, the soft glow of the bedside lamp illuminating her thoughtful expression. With a gentle touch, she traced the delicate outline of the locket resting against her collarbone, its cool metal a comforting reminder of cherished memories. The house was eerily quiet, the usual sounds of creaking wood and distant traffic absent, as if the world outside had paused in reverence to the turmoil of the last few days. A heavy sense of introspection settled within her, weighing on her chest like a thick fog.

With a deep breath, she flipped open her worn leather journal, its pages filled with scribbles and sketches that echoed her innermost thoughts. As she pressed the pen to the blank page, her hand hesitated for a moment, capturing the swirl of emotions that churned within her. The ink finally flowed a steady release of the pent-up feelings she had kept at bay, one word at a time.

June 28

Today, my father almost died. The panic attack was so

bad my mom thought his heart was failing. That should terrify me. And it does.

But today was also the day my parents decided that this last summer—would be the best of my life. And I realize now that I have a choice.

I can sit in this bed, let time pass me by, or make it mean something. I am tired and weak, but I am still here. So, I will take whatever time I have left and fill it with love —with Graham, my parents, laughter, memories, and warmth. I will not wait for the end. I will live.

She set the journal aside and exhaled slowly, her fingers brushing the locket again. She was still here. And she wasn't going to waste a second more.

Chapter Twelve: Promises in the Time We Have

Willow stared at the spreadsheet in front of her, the numbers blurring together as her mind wandered. She had been at work for hours but hadn't been present. Her body was here, her fingers moving mechanically over the keyboard, but her heart was miles away, sitting beside Naomi's bed, watching over her, making sure she was okay. She exhaled, tapping her fingers against the desk, fighting the urge to grab her phone and call. What if she's having a bad day? What if the pain is worse? What if she's just too exhausted even to pick up the phone?

The thoughts coiled in her stomach like a fist, tightening with every passing second. She hated being away. Naomi would tell her not to worry and to live her life, but how was she supposed to when she felt like time was slipping away?

Her gaze flicked to the window, and in an instant, she was transported back to being seventeen again. The warm breeze of summer swept through the open space, carrying with it the faint scent of salt and sunscreen. The rhythmic sound of waves crashing against the shore filled her ears, creating a backdrop to the memory. She could almost hear the joyous peal of Naomi's laughter—it was light and carefree, echoing like a melody of youth. They had rented a small, weathered sailboat from the bustling marina, its bright blue hull contrasting with the soft golden sands. Neither of them had ever set foot on a sailboat before; their sailing knowledge was limited to movies and vague anecdotes from friends. Yet, they were young and invincible at that moment, fueled by an intoxicating sense of adventure and the belief that they could conquer the open sea. With barely a plan, they had eagerly hoisted the sail, their faces alight with excitement and apprehension, convinced that the wind would guide them just as their dreams did.

"You said you knew how to do this!" Willow had screeched as the boat tilted dangerously.

"I thought I did!" Naomi had shouted back, gripping the ropes with both hands, her laughter bubbling even as they fought to keep the boat steady.

They had nearly flipped over at least five times as the waves crashed around them, the boat teetering on the edge of disaster before finally returning to shore. Soaked from head to toe, breathless from the adrenaline, and laughing so hard their sides ached, it had been one of the best days of their lives—filled with carefree joy and the thrill of adventure—before life became a tangled web of complications. The shadows of sickness crept in, stealing laughter from their conversations before the painful goodbyes that lingered long after the words had been spoken. Willow blinked, bringing herself back to the present with a tightness in her throat that felt like a weight.

She reached for her phone, her fingers hovering over Naomi's contact name, longing to hear her familiar voice for a fleeting moment. But hesitation gripped her, and she set the phone down instead, pressing her lips together in a determined silence, wrestling with a heart filled with memories and the ache of absence. Naomi wouldn't want her to worry every second of the day. She would want her to live.

The bell chimed softly as Graham stepped into Sterling Jewelers, his hands shoved deep in his pockets. He hadn't been here in ten years. The last time, he and Naomi had wandered in just for fun, laughing as they pointed out rings, talking about forever like it was inevitable. He was making it a reality

A silver-haired woman named Marla Jacobs stepped gracefully toward him, her kind, twinkling eyes radiating warmth that enveloped him like a cozy blanket. The soft lines of her face, etched with years of laughter and wisdom, hinted at a well-lived life. She wore a gentle smile that seemed to light up the dim room, and her elegant attire—a pastel cardigan draped over a floral blouse—added a touch of cheerful color to her presence.

"Looking for something special?" she asked.

Graham cleared his throat, nodding. "Yeah. An engagement ring."

Marla's smile deepened. "Well, let's make sure it's perfect, then."

He barely needed to look as his heart raced at the sight before him. There it was, gleaming under the softly diffused light—an exquisite two-carat marquise diamond set in a delicate band of white gold that shimmered like a cascade of stars. The diamond's elongated shape caught the light from every angle, casting playful reflections on the surface around it. He could almost hear the echoes of the past when Naomi had stood beside him, her eyes sparkling with delight. It was a moment etched in his memory, one where she had reached out to touch the glittering jewel and whispered, "This is the one," her voice barely above a breath. In that instant, they shared a dream of forever, and as he now gazed at the ring, all the emotions of that day flooded back—the promise, the love, and the hope for a future together.

Graham reached for it, his chest tightening.

"This is the one!" he said with excitement.

Marla nodded. "She's a lucky woman."

He was the lucky one, or at least that's what he kept telling himself as he stood at the counter. As he swiped his card, his hands trembled slightly—not from nerves, but from the anticipation that coursed through him. He had never been more sure of anything in his life. With every heartbeat, the reality of what he would do settled deeper within him. Naomi would be his wife. He was sure of it, no matter how long they had left together. As he took the receipt from the cashier, he clenched it tightly, a tangible symbol of a promise he was ready to make.

At Jameson & Co. Woodworks, the warm, inviting aroma of freshly cut timber filled the air as Beck sat at his rustic wooden desk, rubbing his temples in frustration. The late afternoon sun streamed through the workshop's large windows, casting a golden hue across the array of blueprints and woodworking tools scattered around him. Hiring someone new wasn't the challenge; it was the crucial task of finding the right person to blend seamlessly into the company's creative ethos. One by one, candidates in crisp resumes and their best professional attire filed into the room, their footsteps echoing slightly on the polished floor, looking hopeful and eager yet apprehensive as they faced the daunting task of impressing Beck.

Eric Morrison, 32, stands tall with broad shoulders that give him a commanding presence. His serious demeanor is accentuated by deep-set, thoughtful eyes that reflect determination and a hint of introspection. His close-cropped dark hair is speckled with the first signs of gray, adding a touch of maturity to his rugged appearance. Dressed in a fitted navy blue shirt and dark jeans, he exudes confidence and purpose, suggesting a man accustomed to facing challenges head-on.

"I've been working with wood since I was sixteen," he said, arms crossed. "I build for the long haul, not shortcuts."

Beck nodded. "You sound like our kind of guy."

Jake Sullivan, a 25-year-old with a laid-back demeanor, possesses a rugged charm that truly sets him apart in any crowd. His tousled dark hair often falls casually over his forehead, framing a face that lights up with a warm and inviting smile. This easygoing attitude makes him approachable, drawing people in effortlessly. However, beneath his relaxed exterior lies a depth of character that reveals itself in moments of truth. He has a strong sense of conviction and is unafraid to voice his opinions, tackling challenging situations with a blend of honesty and tact.

"I may not have the most experience," he admitted, "but I promise, I'll work harder than anyone you've ever met."

Beck raised an eyebrow. "That's a bold claim."

Jake grinned. "Give me a block of wood, and I'll prove it."

Trevor Daniels, a 40-year-old man, possesses a quiet demeanor that often masks his inner confidence. With an easygoing smile and an observant nature, he navigates through life with a calm assurance that draws people to him. His thoughtful insights and ability to remain composed in challenging situations reveal a depth of character that few fully appreciate at first glance.

"I've been running my shop," he explained, "but with a wife and two kids, I need something steady."

Beck studied his résumé. "You'd have to learn how we do things here."

Trevor nodded. "I can do that."

Anthony Diaz, a 29-year-old with a brash demeanor, exudes an air of cockiness that often borders on overconfidence. With a sharp jawline and piercing blue eyes, he navigates social and professional settings as if he owns them, often relying on his quick wit and charisma to charm those around him. His bold personality draws attention and thrives on admiration, sometimes failing to recognize when he pushes others' boundaries. Driven by ambition, Anthony's self-assuredness can lead to remarkable achievements and equally significant missteps, illustrating the fine line between confidence and hubris.

"I can build anything," he boasted.

Beck leaned back. "We don't need a magician. We need a craftsman."

Anthony smirked. "Then you're looking at the best."

A 22-year-old trade school graduate, Miles Harper, stood at the crossroads of excitement and anxiety. With a toolbox slung over his shoulder and a head full of dreams, he was keen to embark on a career in carpentry. The scent of fresh wood and the roar of power tools filled his mind with visions of crafting beautiful furniture and building sturdy homes. Though his hands were skilled from hours of practice, uncertainty hovered over him as he prepared to step into the professional world for the first time. Determined to prove himself, Miles was ready to tackle the challenges and opportunities ahead.

"I... uh, I love woodworking," he stammered. "It's—it's my passion."

Beck nodded. "Passion's good. Can you back it up with skill?"

Miles chuckled nervously. "That's what I'm here to prove."

Beck leaned back in his chair, a deep sigh escaping his lips as he gazed out the window at the fading twilight. The options before him were solid, each promising a sense of purpose. Yet, despite the array of choices, his thoughts kept drifting back to Naomi. It had been months since he'd last laid eyes on her, a fleeting moment swallowed by the shadows of her illness. He hadn't visited, choosing instead to keep his distance, wrestling with the mixed emotions that stirred within him. His resentment lingered like a heavy fog, rooted in the memories of what she had done to Graham all those years ago—a betrayal that had shattered their friendship and Beck's faith in people. But tonight was different. Tonight, he would set aside their bitterness and confront the truth of their fractured past. He would see her and, perhaps, find a way to navigate the tangled web of forgiveness.

Thomas sat at the kitchen table, the warm light of the morning sun streaming through the window, illuminating the steam rising from his coffee cup. His fingers traced the chipped edge of the ceramic, a testament to the countless mornings it had seen. Beside him, Ruth sat with her hair pulled back in a loose bun, her brow furrowed in concentration as she flipped through the pages of her notepad. It was filled with a jumble of notes and doodles, evidence of her thoughts racing ahead. The faint scent of freshly brewed coffee mingled with the sweet aroma of cinnamon from the breakfast pastries on the counter, creating an inviting atmosphere for their conversation.

"We need a plan," she said softly. "To make this summer special for her."

Thomas exhaled, rubbing his temples. "What does she love?"

Slowly, they began to write a list to make their daughter's last summer with them a beautiful memory instead of the most heartbreaking loss of their lives.

• A sunset picnic by the shore.
• A bonfire night with close friends.
• A day of painting on the porch.
• A surprise dinner with all her favorite foods.
• One last perfect day—whatever she wants.

Thomas swallowed hard, his emotions constricting his throat, leaving his voice thick and unsteady.

"We can't make this okay," he said, his eyes filled with despair and resignation.

Ruth turned to him, her hand reaching out to find his, her fingers wrapping around his reassuringly. She squeezed gently, her touch warm and steady amidst the cold uncertainty surrounding them.

"No," she replied softly, her voice soothingly against the turmoil. "But we can make it beautiful." She offered him a small, hopeful smile to suggest that there was still the potential for grace and meaning even in the face of hardship.

He nodded, his brow furrowing slightly as he felt the familiar tension coil in his chest. With a steady hand, he reached for the small amber bottle of anti-anxiety pills sitting on the cluttered table beside him. The bottle felt cool against his palm, a reassuring sensation amid his rising unease. He twisted off the cap, carefully shaking out one pale blue tablet, its surface gleaming under the dim light. He swallowed it, and the bitter taste lingered in his mouth. He took a deep breath, summoning all the courage he could muster. He needed to be strong for her and the pillar of support she relied on during this turbulent time.

The engagement ring rested in the deep black velvet box that sat invitingly on the passenger seat of Graham's aging pickup truck. With his fingers tightly curled around the leather-wrapped steering wheel, he felt his pulse quicken. He inhaled slowly, filling his lungs with the warm evening air as the sun descended, casting a golden hue over everything it touched.

This was the moment he had been waiting for, and he felt a surge of determination wash over him. No more hesitation, no more dwelling on the "what-ifs." The only thing that mattered now was the woman he loved and making her his wife, no matter how few tomorrows they might have left.

With a newfound resolve, he unbuckled his seatbelt and swung open the truck door, the scent of wildflowers and freshly cut grass wafting toward him. He tucked the velvet box securely into his jacket pocket, feeling its weight against his side, a tangible reminder of the commitment he was about to make.

He stepped out into the warm, salty air, his heart racing as he approached Naomi's front porch, each step bringing him closer to the love of his life. She had always been the one—the laughter in his darkest days, the calm in his chaos. Today, he would finally express his feelings and ask her to be by his side forever. With every breath, he felt the anticipation build, knowing he was stepping into a future he had always dreamed of with the woman he had loved for over a decade.

Chapter Thirteen: The Proposal

The evening sky unfolded like a breathtaking canvas, awash with warm hues that blended seamlessly; molten gold flowed into soft lavender, punctuated by vibrant streaks of fiery orange that seemed to dance across the horizon. A gentle breeze whispered through the air, laced with the briny scent of the nearby ocean, wrapping Naomi in a comforting embrace of quiet serenity. She sat nestled in a weathered wooden chair on her porch, a cozy knitted blanket—patterns of rich burgundy and deep teal—draped over her lap. As she gazed into the horizon, each color shift in the sky captivated her, transforming the mundane into the extraordinary. Even on the most challenging days, the sunsets offered an unwavering beauty, a reminder of nature's artistry that always managed to soothe her weary soul.

Then she heard the low rumble of his truck pulling into the gravel driveway, the sound sweeping over her like a warm wave. The familiar noise settled something deep within her chest, banishing the tension that had lingered throughout the day. Naomi had always had an uncanny knack for sensing when Graham would arrive; it was as if an invisible thread connected them, always pulling tighter just before he showed up.

As he stepped out of the truck, his shoes thudded

against the weathered porch steps, each sound echoing in the crisp evening air. The way his jaw clenched slightly, a muscle twitching with apprehension, revealed his nerves—an emotion that belied his usual confident demeanor. His shoulders squared as he stepped closer, a protective instinct that seemed to surface in unfamiliar situations as if he were bracing himself for whatever awaited him inside.

"You always find me out here," she murmured without looking at him.

"I always will," he said softly.

He carefully lowered himself into the worn chair beside her. Their hands rested close together on the small table, fingertips almost grazing but never quite making contact. The silence enveloped them wasn't empty; it was rich with meaning, weighted and warm. Each moment shimmered with everything unspoken between them—an echo of their enduring love, the bittersweet memories of their shared past, the years that slipped away like sand through their fingers, and the precious time that stretched before them, fragile and fleeting.

Naomi exhaled slowly. "I was thinking about us today."

Graham turned toward her. His curiosity was piqued as he studied the delicate arch of her profile and how the sunlight caught the strands of her hair. He noted the slight furrow in her brow, hinting at the thoughts swirling within her mind, and he could almost hear the unspoken words hanging in the air. He waited patiently, his gaze fixed on her, eager for her to continue and reveal what was weighing on her heart.

"How we used to dream about the future," she said, "like we had all the time in the world. Like nothing could touch us."

He let out a chuckle. "We were very young."

"Naïve is who we were back then."

Graham's voice softened. "Maybe. But we weren't wrong about everything."

Naomi lifted her gaze to his, her brow furrowing slightly. "What do you mean?"

He hesitated briefly, his heart pounding like a drum as he reached into the depths of his pocket, fingers brushing against the fabric. Finally, he pulled out a small velvet box, its rich, dark blue surface shimmering under the soft glow of the lights.

Naomi's breath caught in her throat, a rush of anticipation mingling with surprise flooding her senses. Graham turned toward her, his striking blue eyes reflecting a whirlwind of emotions—fear of the unknown, the warmth of love wrapped around them like a familiar blanket, and the certainty that this moment was pivotal in their lives.

"This moment is one I have been waiting for a long time," he said, flipping open the box and revealing a two-carat white gold marquise diamond ring. The same one she had once admired in a shop window ten years ago before everything fell apart. Her hand flew to her mouth as tears immediately welled in her eyes.

"Graham..." her voice cracked, shaking with emotion.

"I should have given this to you a long time ago," he murmured. "But I don't care how many days we have left. I don't care what tomorrow brings. I know I want them with you."

A soft sob escaped her lips, trembling with the weight of unspoken emotions, as he gently reached for her hand. His warm thumb brushed over her delicate, trembling fingers, sending a shiver of comfort mixed with vulnerability through her. The contrast of his steady touch against her quaking grip spoke volumes in the moment's silence, a silent promise of understanding and support amidst the turmoil swirling in her heart.

"Naomi, I don't need forever," he whispered. "I just need you."

Her chest ached, a heavy, throbbing sensation that felt both full and as if it were about to shatter. Each breath was a struggle, like her heart were a fragile glass orb, teetering on the edge of breaking, caught in a tempest of conflicting emotions.

"I—I don't know if I can do this to you," she admitted, tears slipping down her cheeks. "I don't want to be your heartbreak, Graham. I don't want to leave you with just a memory."

He shook his head, his brow furrowing in frustration as he gripped her hand tighter, feeling the warmth of her skin beneath his fingers. The weight of unspoken words hung between them, making the moment feel urgent and heavy.

"You're not just a memory," he said fiercely. "You are everything. And I don't care if we get years or weeks or just one hour. I want every second I can have with you."

Naomi let out a shaky breath, her heart pounding as she stared at the ring glimmering in the soft light. The delicate band, adorned with intricate filigree and a sparkling, oval-shaped diamond, caught her eye, drawing her in deeper. It would be so easy to say no, to push him away and shield him from the inevitable pain that loomed on the horizon. She could hear her own voice echoing in her mind, a warning against the heartache that seemed insurmountable.

But he was right. In that moment, love wasn't merely about the amount of time they had spent together; it was about the conscious choice to embrace vulnerability, to lean into the uncertainty of their future. With a surge of emotion, she realized that she had made her decision long before this moment. She chose him—every laugh they shared, every quiet evening spent in each other's company, and every challenge they had faced together.

A slow, tearful smile spread across her lips as she looked up at him, her eyes glistening with unshed tears. She could see the hope in his gaze and the reassurance that he would be there for her through it all. In that instance, surrounded by the warm glow of their shared memories, she felt an overwhelming sense of clarity and love.

"I don't need forever either," she whispered. "I just need you."

A choked sound escaped his throat as he carefully slipped the delicate silver ring onto her finger, feeling the cool metal settle into a place where it had always belonged. The ring fits perfectly, its intricate design catching the light like a promise of eternal love. As he leaned in closer, the warmth of his breath mingled with the sweet scent of her hair, and he pressed a soft, reverent kiss against her lips. In that fleeting moment, with their hearts racing in sync, Naomi finally let herself believe in something greater than the ticking clock of her remaining time—a hope that sparkled like the stars in the vast night sky, illuminating a future they could dream of together.

The soft, rhythmic knock at the door took Naomi by

surprise. She had barely begun to process the whirlwind of emotions that accompanied her recent engagement when the sound pierced the quiet evening. Graham had just stepped inside to grab a drink, leaving her alone on the porch with the comforting weight of a soft, navy-blue blanket wrapped around her shoulders.

Curiosity bubbled within her as she stood up, glancing back into the dimly lit room where faint laughter and clinking glasses echoed. The cool breeze sent a shiver through her, urging her to pull the blanket tighter. With a deep breath, she opened the door.

Her heart skipped a beat as she saw him. Beck stood with a hesitant figure framed by the warm glow of the porch light. His hands were buried deep in the pockets of his jeans, and he shifted his weight awkwardly from one foot to the other as if unsure whether to take a step forward or retreat. The uncertain look on his face tugged at her heartstrings, stirring memories of laughter and late-night conversations that felt like a lifetime ago.

"Beck," she whispered, blinking in surprise.

His gaze flickered, hesitating as though he were carefully assembling his thoughts, each word a fragile thread waiting to be woven into the fabric of their conversation. He finally locked eyes with hers again, the tension between them palpable in the charged silence.

"I, uh…" He cleared his throat. "I wasn't sure if I should come."

Naomi's heart squeezed painfully.

"But you did," she said softly.

Beck nodded once. "Yeah. I did."

She stepped aside. "Come in."

He hesitated before stepping over the threshold, his stance tense, like a man carrying old wounds that hadn't healed. They stood in the quiet for a moment before Naomi broke it.

"You've been avoiding me."

Beck exhaled sharply, running a hand over his face. "Not avoiding. Just…" He let out a tired laugh. "I was angry, Naomi, for a long time. When you left, Graham—he wasn't the same. And I guess I blamed you for that."

She swallowed past the lump in her throat. "I know."

Beck shook his head. "And I held onto that for too long. But now…" His voice lowered, more raw than she had ever heard it. "None of it matters anymore."

Naomi's throat tightened. "Beck…"

He glanced toward the porch, where Graham had just stood minutes ago.

"I see the way he looks at you," Beck murmured. "And I just… I want him to be happy. And you, too."

Tears pricked her eyes.

"I never stopped loving him," she admitted. "Even when I walked away."

Beck let out a slow breath before nodding.

"I know."

And just like that, the sharp edges of their resentment began to soften into something gentler—something resembling understanding. The air between them seemed to shift, the tense silence replaced by an unspoken acknowledgment of their shared struggle. Before he stepped through the door, he paused, glancing over his shoulder. A hint of a smirk played at the corners of his lips, a fleeting gesture that hinted at a newfound camaraderie amidst their complicated history.

"Don't break his heart this time, okay?"

Naomi smiled through her tears. "I won't."

The backyard glowed warmly beneath a canopy of

twinkling fairy lights, their soft illumination casting a magical shimmer over everything. The gentle melodies of a classic acoustic guitar drifted softly through the warm evening air, mingling with the sweet scent of blooming jasmine. Naomi sat at the rustic wooden table, her heart swelling with joy as she watched the faces of the people she cherished most—friends and family—laughing and chatting animatedly. Their voices blended into a harmonious symphony of affection, each smile and shared glance a testament to the bonds they held. The tables were adorned with vibrant centerpieces of wildflowers, and the gentle rustling of leaves above added to the enchanting atmosphere, creating a perfect moment of connection and warmth.

Her father, Thomas, reached for her hand, squeezing gently.

"Dance with me?" he asked, his voice gruff with emotion.

Naomi hesitated before letting him pull her up.

He moved slow, careful, steadying her when her strength wavered.

"You okay?" he whispered.

She smiled against his shoulder, blinking back tears.

"I am now."

Later, as Graham pulled her into his arms, resting his chin against her head, she whispered, "I want to marry you soon."

Graham pressed a soft kiss to her forehead.

"Then tell me when," he said with a smile. "And it's done."

Naomi opened her journal to write about a beautiful day.

June 30

Tonight, I was alive. For the first time in so long, I didn't think about what I was losing. I didn't think about the days I won't have, the future I won't see. I just... existed. I danced with my father, laughed with my friends, and kissed the man who has loved me through it all. If love could keep me here, I'd never leave. But love is not about time. It's about what we do with the time we have. And tonight, I was alive.

Chapter Fourteen: In Light and Love

It was the second of July, and the rich aroma of freshly brewed coffee wafted through the air, mingling delightfully with the salty breeze that spilled through the open windows of Seabreeze Café. This sun-washed corner spot, just steps from the golden shoreline of Cape May, had long been a cherished haven for locals. Inside, writers huddled over their journals. Their brows furrowed in concentration as they penned their thoughts while barefoot couples shared soft laughter, sipping creamy lattes topped with delicate froth art. In one corner, older men with silver hair and reading glasses perched low on their noses leafed through well-worn newspapers, the sharp aroma of black coffee steaming beside them—its rich flavor a companion to their morning ritual.

The café, adorned with pale blue shutters that creaked gently in the breeze and driftwood signs artfully hanging from strings, welcomed guests with an inviting charm that radiated from its cozy interior. Today, however, the atmosphere felt imbued with an unspoken tension, a sense that something tender, sacred, and just a little bit urgent was about to unfold within those familiar walls. The sun's warmth filtered through the windows, casting a golden hue on the worn wooden tables, where the stories of countless individuals had been exchanged over cups of comfort. As patrons settled in, laughter and the clinking of cups created a symphony of everyday life, setting the stage for an encounter that would be far from ordinary.

Ruth sat at a small, wrought-iron table by the window, her fingers gently wrapped around a steaming mug of chamomile tea, its floral aroma filling the air with a sense of calm. The morning sun filtered through the sheer white curtains, casting a gentle glow on her worn notepad, already smudged with inked thoughts—words like "dress," "flowers," and "location" jumbled across the page, each one promising a future filled with memories yet unwritten.

Across from her, Willow settled into the chair with a heavy sigh, echoing the weight of her unspoken emotions. She tucked a loose strand of her dark hair behind her ear, her fingers trembling slightly as they brushed against her cheek, revealing the faint traces of tears that glistened in her eyes. In that moment, she embodied the essence of grief: graceful in her presence but undeniably worn, as though the immense weight of love had softened her spirit and left her heart fragile—a delicate balance of sorrow and beauty.

"I can't believe we're doing this," Willow said softly, pulling her iced coffee closer. "A wedding. In four days."

Ruth's smile was small but full of meaning. "We're giving her something joyful to hold onto. Something beautiful. Even now."

They fell quiet momentarily as the sea breeze danced over the tabletop, lifting the corner of Ruth's notes.

"I was thinking," Willow began, a bit of color rising to her cheeks, "about this boutique—Tide & Thread. It's tucked right behind the old lighthouse. Naomi and I went there years ago, and she tried on this light blue sundress. She said it reminded her of the sky right before it rains." She smiled at the memory. "She loved that color."

"She still does," Ruth said. "Blue has always been hers."

Willow nodded, eyes welling. "Then let her wear it. Something soft, flowy. She'll look like the tide itself."

Ruth reached for her phone, her fingers trembling slightly as she dialed Graham. He answered on the second ring.

"Hey," he said, his voice already thick with emotion.

Willow leaned in closer to Ruth, her voice barely above a whisper. "July sixth, remember? Cape May, right at sunset. Naomi will wear that stunning blue dress with the delicate lace trim."

There was a pause, then a long breath on the other end. "It's perfect," Graham said. "It's her."

Ruth added gently, "She always dreamed of marrying you by the water. Even as a little girl, she said her wedding would have waves nearby."

Graham chuckled softly. "I'll meet her at the edge of the ocean. I promise."

Before they hung up, he added, "Please arrange for eight beautiful roses, a perfect blend of blue and white. This specific combination has always been her dream—a striking contrast that captivates the eye and symbolizes the balance between passion and tranquility. Each rose should be fresh and fragrant, embodying the elegance she adores. It's a thoughtful tribute to what she has always desired."

"We'll make it happen," Ruth assured him. "Every detail."

"She's going to be a bride," Willow whispered. "Even if just for a moment."

Ruth folded her hands. "And we're going to make it feel like forever."

That same morning, across town, the air was thick with the invigorating scent of freshly cut lumber, mingling seamlessly with the soft, constant hum of machines at work, creating a harmonious backdrop in the expansive space of Jameson & Co. Woodworks. Beck stood poised in the rustic wooden doorway of his office, his lean frame casting a shadow as he observed his committed crew with an appreciative eye. They were engrossed in their craft, expertly smoothing the rough edges of rich, aromatic cedar and artistically shaping premium maple into masterpieces that would soon find their place in homes and businesses alike. The golden sunlight poured through large, dust-speckled windows, illuminating the shimmering grains of wood and painting the workshop with a warm, inviting glow.

On his sturdy oak desk, a small, neatly organized stack of résumés sat patiently, each sheet a testament to ambition and aspirations. Considering each candidate's qualifications with great care, Beck had poured over them all, yet only one name lingered in his thoughts: Miles Harper. He was twenty-two and had recently emerged from a respected trade school, filled with excitement and earnestness about the craftsmanship he hoped to pursue. During the interview, he exhibited quiet confidence; he chose his words carefully, each resonating with thoughtfulness rather than haste. His lean, wiry build spoke of hard work and dedication. Dark blond hair curled slightly at the ends, framing a face embodying youth and determination. His hands, rough and calloused from hours of labor, bore the marks of someone deeply engaged in woodworking, hinting at a lifetime spent honing his skills and nurturing a passion for the trade that Beck hoped would bring innovation and craftsmanship to his team.

"I've wanted to build things since I was a kid," he'd said, almost nervously. "Not just to work with my hands—but to leave something behind. Something that stays after I'm gone."

That line had lingered in Beck's mind long after it was spoken—days of contemplation and reflection. As he stood in the dimly lit office, feeling the weight of Graham's departure, it became painfully clear that he required more than just assistance; he needed someone who possessed heart and integrity, a steadfast ally to mentor and nurture. Trust was essential, especially in these trying circumstances. With determination brewing in his chest, he picked up the phone, his fingers hovering over the numbers momentarily as he steeled himself for what lay ahead.

"Miles?" Beck asked once the young man answered. "You free to start Monday morning? Seven sharp?"

There was a beat of surprised silence, followed by a smile Beck could almost hear. "Yes, sir. Thank you."

Beck hung up and looked around the shop.

He thought, " One more accomplishment checked off the list," feeling a sense of fulfillment—for Graham, for the ones we cherish.

Later that afternoon, Ruth and Willow navigated into the historic district of Cape May, their car gliding along the cobblestone streets that seemed to whisper tales of the past. Mariner's Lane felt like a scene from a bygone era—charming wooden signs creaked softly in the gentle breeze while window boxes overflowed with vibrant, blooming geraniums and delicate petunias. Locals strolled, some cradling cone-shaped bouquets of fragrant lavender, its sweet scent mingling with the salty air, while others sported tote bags adorned with colorful seashells, evidence of a perfect day spent by the shore. The golden afternoon sunlight cast a warm glow, illuminating the intricate gingerbread trim of the historic Victorian homes, each telling its own story of heritage and community.

They parked beside a white building draped in climbing roses and stepped into Bloom & Tide, the scent of blossoms wrapping around them like silk. A woman appeared behind a counter, her hands dusted with pollen and her braid draped over one shoulder. The floral shop owner, Clara Bennett, gave them a soft, knowing smile.

"We need a bridal bouquet," Ruth said. "For a wedding on the beach."

Clara's eyes lit up with understanding as if she sensed the deeper story behind the request.

"Blue and white roses," Willow added. "Something delicate. Something that feels like her."

Clara led them to the worktable near the back, where glass vases lined the shelves like treasures. She pulled out a few stems and laid them on soft tissue.

"How about five blue roses," Clara murmured, "three white, woven with baby's breath. We'll trim the stems and wrap them in white silk. No extras. No distractions. Just her colors and her light."

Willow placed a hand over her mouth, her eyes brimming.

"It'll be breathtaking," Clara said. "I promise."

As evening descended, the light transformed into a

warm golden hue, enveloping Cape May in a serene glow. Naomi sat curled up on the porch, wrapped in a cozy, hand-knit blanket harmonizing beautifully with the soft blues and creams of the weathered wicker furniture. The gentle swing of an old rocking chair, its paint chipped from years of use, creaked softly in sync with the whisper of the evening breeze.

Beside her, a white, weathered table bore the weight of her well-loved journal, its pages filled with heartfelt musings and whimsical sketches—each mark a testament to her introspective journey. A crystal glass glinted in the waning light, filled with freshly squeezed orange juice that glimmered like sunlight captured in liquid form. Nearby, the delicate silver ring that Graham had slipped onto her finger sparkled softly, its intricate design catching the day's last rays.

The distant cries of seagulls overhead gradually faded into the soothing symphony of waves crashing rhythmically against the shore. Their surf lapped at the sand with a gentle, almost musical cadence, creating a perfect backdrop for her moment of quiet reflection. The air was tinged with the briny scent of the ocean, and Naomi closed her eyes, letting the sounds and scents wash over her, savoring the tranquility of this golden hour.

Graham returned from his call, balancing a small wooden tray with an elegant assortment of finely sliced artisanal cheeses, including a creamy brie, sharp aged cheddar, and tangy blue cheese. Beside them lay delicate slices of prosciutto and salami, their rich colors inviting interest. Interspersed among the meats were crunchy, golden-brown crackers that added a satisfying texture, while plump, juicy grapes and vibrant wedges of ripe apple offered a refreshing contrast. The tray was carefully arranged, and each element was thoughtfully placed to create a visually appealing and mouthwatering presentation.

"You didn't have to do all this," Naomi said, reaching for a piece of pear.

"I know," Graham replied, sitting beside her. "But I wanted to. You're the bride. It's your week."

She smiled softly, a tired but radiant glow enhancing her features. Her fingers delicately brushed against his as she absentmindedly picked at the food on her plate. Her appetite was light yet consistent, betraying a hunger for something more than just nourishment. The cool evening breeze danced around them, playfully tugging at the frayed edges of her blanket, which draped softly over her shoulders, adding a cozy warmth against the chill of the night air.

"I heard it's official," she said, glancing sideways at him. "July sixth."

"Four days from now," he said. "I'll be the luckiest groom on this coast."

Naomi leaned her head on his shoulder. "It's all happening so fast."

He kissed the top of her head. "Sometimes fast is beautiful too."

They sat together in silence, her hand resting over his heart.

"It's going to be a beautiful wedding," she whispered. "Even if it's only us and the sea."

Graham pulled her closer. "It already is."

That night, Ruth stood at the kitchen window, holding the phone to her ear as the house grew quiet behind her.

"Thank you again," she said. "It means more than I can say."

The voice on the other end was warm and kind. Pastor Eli Whitcomb, from Grace by the Sea Chapel, had agreed to officiate the ceremony.

"I'd like to meet the couple first," he said gently. "Just to hear their hearts. A wedding—especially one like this—is sacred."

"They'll be ready," Ruth promised.

A sense of calm washed over her as she hung up the phone. Her eyes were drawn to the expansive sky, where the moon hung low on the horizon, its luminous face revealing craters and shadows that told a silent story. It cast a shimmering silver path across the tranquil water, each ripple reflecting the moonlight like scattered diamonds, always guiding the gaze back to the sandy shore. The gentle lapping of the waves created a soothing soundtrack, perfectly harmonizing with the soft night air that kissed her skin, wrapping her in a serene embrace.

Chapter Fifteen: The Weight and Wonder of Love

The overcast morning settled over Cape May like a soft, gray blanket, the air thick with the briny scent of salt and an enveloping silence. Naomi nestled herself into the worn wooden swing on the back porch, wrapping a delicate, pale blue shawl tightly around her shoulders as she sought warmth from the cool sea breeze. Her gaze drifted to the churning waves just beyond the dune grass, where patches of golden sand peeked through the lush green blades. The rhythmic crash of the surf was steady and reassuring, a familiar melody that had offered her comfort and solace since childhood. She could almost hear the whispers of the sea, echoing the memories of laughter and carefree days spent building castles in the sand and collecting seashells along the shore. She reached for her journal, resting it across her knees. Her fingers trembled slightly, but the pen found the paper.

July 3

The sea doesn't mourn like we do. It keeps breathing, rising, falling—faithfully. I used to believe love had to roar. Now I know it can whisper and still be valid. Today, I just want to be here. At this moment. In this breath. Still his. The screen door creaked behind her. Graham stepped onto the porch carrying a small plate of toast and honey.

"Didn't think you'd eaten," he said softly.

Naomi glanced at him, a weak smile forming. "You know me too well."

He handed her the plate, sitting beside her. Their shoulders touched, his warmth grounding her.

"I like watching you write," he said. "It makes me feel like the world is still moving."

"It is," she whispered. "Even if I'm moving slower."

He kissed her. "We'll move slower together."

The rich, earthy scent of cedar enveloped the workshop at Jameson & Co. Woodworks, creating an inviting atmosphere that spoke of craftsmanship and dedication. Sunlight streamed through the large, dusty windows, casting warm, golden rays on the long plank of red cedar that lay on the workbench before Graham and Beck. The grain of the wood was a stunning tapestry of soft reddish-brown hues, its surface smooth to the touch, polished by countless hours of labor. As Graham carefully examined the delicate carvings etched into the wood, each stroke revealed stories of nature and artistry, harmoniously blending together in a design that felt both authentic and timeless. Beck stood beside him, his brow furrowed in concentration as he contemplated the next steps in their creation, the air around them humming with possibility and the promise of craftsmanship.

Graham and Naomi Jameson

July 6, 2024

"She's going to cry when she sees this," Beck said, wiping his hands with a cloth.

Graham traced his finger along the final line. "I hope she does. I want her to feel every bit of how loved she is."

Beck leaned against the worktable. "You've changed, you know."

"How so?"

"You're softer. But stronger, too. Like you've finally stopped guarding your heart."

Graham shrugged. "I didn't know how much I had to give until she returned."

"Funny," Beck said. "I always thought you were waiting for her."

"I was," Graham admitted. "Even when I told myself I wasn't."

Beck nudged him gently. "You're a better man because of her. And that's the kind of love worth carving into wood."

In her small, dimly lit apartment, Hanna methodically zipped her suitcase shut, the sound of the zipper breaking the heavy silence that enveloped her. She sat on the edge of the bed, its unmade sheets rumpled beneath her, and glanced around the room. The faded photographs on the walls captured moments of laughter and love, but now they felt like haunted reminders, echoing with unspoken goodbyes.

Each item in the room—the worn-out armchair in the corner, the half-empty bookshelf crammed with well-thumbed novels—seemed to vibrate with the weight of her memories, which were too sharp and vivid to bear. Her heart ached with the finality of leaving as the realization settled that her time in this space was ending. Bar Harbor would be a clean slate.

A gentle knock echoed through the room, breaking the silence. Ezra then peeked in through the door with a slight smile as he carefully balanced two steaming cups of coffee in his hands. The rich, aromatic scent of freshly brewed coffee filled the air, hinting at the warmth and comfort they would bring this remarkable morning.

"I brought the essentials," he said, placing one on her nightstand.

"You sure you're up for a spontaneous relocation?" she asked with a raised brow.

"I'm up for healing. And you need someone who reminds you how powerful you are when you forget."

She exhaled. "I thought I could handle this—watching him marry her."

"And you could," Ezra said. "But surviving isn't the same as living."

She gave a half-smile. "Thank you for not saying something cliché."

"Oh, give me time," he teased. "We've got a long road trip ahead."

Back at the quaint little shop adorned with colorful flower boxes under the windows, Beck stepped outside into the cool afternoon breeze. The sun cast a warm glow on the cobblestone street as he pulled out his phone and dialed Miles Harper, hoping to catch him before the busy evening rush began.

"Beck Jameson here," he said when Miles answered.

"Sir! I—I was hoping you'd call."

"Congratulations, kid! You're officially hired for the position. Your first day will be this coming Monday at 7 AM sharp. Be ready to hit the ground running and bring your best attitude. We're excited to have you on board!"

There was a stunned pause. "Really? Thank you, sir. Thank you so much. I promise—I won't let you down."

"I don't expect perfection, Miles. I expect honesty and effort. You've got both."

Miles's voice cracked slightly. "I won't waste this."

"Good. We'll see you bright and early."

On the creaking wooden porch, Naomi nestled

comfortably under a soft, thick blanket that enveloped her like a warm cocoon. Golden sunlight filtered through the leaves of the towering oak tree, casting playful shadows around her. Lena Ruiz, her dedicated hospice nurse, diligently adjusted the IV line, and her movements were gentle and practiced. The clear bag of electrolytes swayed slightly in the soft breeze, its contents reflecting the dappled sunlight. The thin, translucent tube snaked securely from the bag to Naomi's arm, ensuring a steady flow of sustenance. Each careful adjustment Lena made carried an air of reassurance, a testament to the bond formed through countless hours of compassionate care.

"You're holding up better than most," Lena said, watching the slow drip.

"I'm stubborn," Naomi said. "And I have something to look forward to."

"Something—or someone?" Lena asked with a knowing smile.

Naomi chuckled. "Both."

Lena took a seat beside her. "Not many people face death with this kind of grace."

Naomi looked out at the ocean. "I don't feel graceful as I navigate through the twists and turns of life. Instead, I feel an overwhelming fear clinging to me like a heavy cloak. Yet, amidst that fear, there's a flicker of determination ignited by my love for him. I want to embrace every precious moment, to live fully until my body can no longer carry me. Every heartbeat echoes my resolve to fight through the shadows, to hold on for him, the light that guides me through the darkness."

"That's all anyone can ask for," Lena said. "To be loved like that—and to leave gently."

Naomi turned to her. "Thank you for treating me

like a person, not a diagnosis."

"You're a soul," Lena said. "The body is just a chapter."

In the softly lit dressing room of Harborlight Clothiers, Ruth stepped inside, clutching a dove-gray dress that shimmered subtly in the light. The fabric was delicate, flowing gracefully as she held it up to admire its elegant lines. Meanwhile, Thomas stood in the adjacent fitting room, adjusting a charcoal suit tailored perfectly to his frame, the sharp lapels enhancing his confident demeanor. When they finally stepped out together, their eyes met, each wearing a watery smile reflecting excitement and vulnerability in this moment of shared anticipation. The atmosphere was filled with a palpable sense of possibility as they stood amidst the soft rustle of fabrics and the faint scent of fresh linen.

"She's going to break our hearts," Thomas said quietly.

"She already has," Ruth replied. "But in the most beautiful way."

They strolled down the sandy path to The Driftwood Grille, a charming seaside eatery known for its relaxed atmosphere. They gazed through the large window as they slid into their familiar booth, upholstered in a faded ocean-blue fabric. The rhythmic sound of waves echoed in the background, their white crests crashing gently against the rugged rocks below, sending up fine salty mist sprays. The sunlight danced on the water's surface, creating a shimmering effect that felt almost magical. The warm breeze carried with it the scent of grilled seafood and the distant laughter of other patrons, enveloping them in a sense of comfort and belonging.

They strolled down the sandy path to The Driftwood Grille, a charming seaside eatery known for its relaxed atmosphere. They gazed through the large window as they slid into their familiar booth, upholstered in a faded ocean-blue fabric. The rhythmic sound of waves echoed in the background, their white crests crashing gently against the rugged rocks below, sending delicate salty mist sprays. The sunlight danced on the water's surface, creating a shimmering effect that felt almost magical. The warm breeze carried with it the scent of grilled seafood and the distant laughter of other patrons, enveloping them in a sense of comfort and belonging.

Thomas stirred his soup, voice low. "I wanted to be her protector. But there's nothing I can do now."

"You're still protecting her," Ruth said. "Every time you sit beside her. Every time you let her be herself."

He blinked rapidly. "She looks so much like you."

Ruth reached across the table. "She has your soul, Thomas. Steady and deep."

Beck leaned against the weathered wood of the porch railing outside the quaint little shop, the scent of freshly baked goods wafting through the air. With a thoughtful expression, he pulled out his phone and dialed his mother, the soft hum of conversation from inside the store mingling with the distant sounds of the bustling street.

"Hey, Mom. How have you been doing?"

"Beck, honey. I'm fine. Is everything okay?"

"Graham's getting married. Saturday, and we need you to be here."

"To Naomi, right?"

"Yeah. Time's short for the two."

A pause. "Then I'm coming and plan to be there for the wedding. I'll stay a while but won't be in the way. Only supportive of my favorite guys."

He smiled. "I figured you would be here for them, well, us."

"I'll stay at the Seacrest Inn. Close enough to be there. Far enough to give everyone their space."

"He'll need you."

"And I'll be ready," Jennifer said. "You boys were always my softest places."

The porch radiated a warm amber light that evening, casting gentle shadows on the wooden floorboards as Pastor Eli Whitcomb settled into his weathered wicker chair across from Naomi and Graham. The air was thick with the scent of blooming jasmine, mingling with the cool breeze that whispered through nearby trees. A well-worn leather Bible rested on his knee, its spine cracked from years of use, yet it remained untouched for the moment as if the weight of the conversation ahead held more significance than the verses within. The soft creaking of the porch and the distant chirping of crickets provided a serene backdrop, enveloping the trio in a cocoon of intimate camaraderie.

"Talk to me," Eli said. "This isn't just about vows. It's about what you're committing to."

Naomi leaned forward. "To live even when it hurts. To let Graham love me when I'm scared."

Graham added, "To walk Naomi home."

Eli nodded slowly. "That's real love—something more profound than what you see in movies. It's not just about grand gestures or dramatic declarations; it's the kind that endures through life's challenges, the quiet moments of understanding, and the unwavering support that lasts beyond time. This is the eternal kind, where two souls are intertwined, sharing laughter in good times and holding each other close in difficult moments, creating an unbreakable bond."

They sat silently for a moment, the quiet enveloping them like a soft blanket. The calm and refreshing wind danced around them gently, rustling the leaves of the nearby trees and carrying the faint scent of blooming wildflowers. Sunlight filtered through the branches above, creating playful patterns of light and shadow on the ground. Each breathed-in moment was filled with a tranquil stillness, inviting reflection, and an undeniable connection to the world around them.

"God doesn't promise time," Eli said. "He promises unwavering presence, a steadfast commitment to being there through every moment, both joyous and challenging. And as you navigate your daily life, you can feel the weight of that assurance, knowing that His support surrounds you, grounding you in the reality of his words. You're already living that promise, experiencing the warmth of companionship and the comfort that comes from knowing someone truly cares."

He opened his Bible and read softly: "Love bears all things, believes all things, hopes all things, endures all things. Love never fails."

Then Psalm 34:18: "The Lord is close to the brokenhearted and saves those who are crushed in spirit."

Eli prayed with unwavering resolve, his voice steady and intentional, each word carefully woven with threads of hope and faith that filled the quiet air around them. The soft glow of the candles flickered softly in the dim room, casting warm shadows on the walls. Naomi, seeking comfort, closed her eyes and let the soothing rhythm of Eli's voice wash over her. She leaned her head gently against Graham's shoulder, feeling the warmth of his presence as a protective balm against her worries. The faint scent of sandalwood lingered in the air, offering peace amidst the uncertainty.

That night, Naomi nestled on the creaky wooden porch, the cool breeze gently rustling the leaves above her. The sky sprawled like a vast canvas, studded with shimmering stars twinkling against the deep indigo backdrop. With her journal resting on her lap, its pages slightly worn from frequent use, she picked up her pen and began to write, the soft glow of a nearby lantern illuminating her thoughts as she poured her heart onto the paper.

July 3 – Night

Pastor Eli said I'm walking through something sacred, that even grief has

holiness. Today, I was witnessed, loved, and listened to. And tomorrow,

I'll rise again—not because I'm strong, but because I'm held.

In the serene neighborhood of Willowcrest Landing, Graham's house sat quietly. It was a charming one-story dwelling painted a muted gray and elegantly accented with crisp white trim that highlighted its simple elegance. The black front door, polished to a shine, welcomed visitors beneath an archway draped with climbing ivy. Surrounding the entrance, clusters of hydrangeas swayed gently in the warm breeze, their vibrant blues and pinks adding a splash of color to the tranquil scene.

Inside, the soft glow of warm, ambient light bathed the open-concept living area, creating a cozy atmosphere.

A plush navy couch adorned with textured pillows invited relaxation, while pale oak wood floors stretched throughout the room, adding a touch of warmth and character. The gentle hum of a nearby ceiling fan stirred the air, mingling with the delicate scent of lavender wafting from a sleek diffuser near the kitchen—a subtle touch that evoked a sense of calm and comfort. The carefully arranged bookshelf, filled with well-worn novels and cherished photo frames, told stories of moments long past, rounding out the inviting space.

Graham and Beck worked side by side in the warm, sunlit kitchen, folding clean and crisp laundry, the faint scent of fabric softener lingering in the air. They meticulously smoothed each shirt and pair of pants, placing them in neat stacks on the table. As they wiped down the counters, the soft sound of cloth on wood filled the space, mingling with the subtle hum of the refrigerator in the background. Fresh towels, fluffy and inviting, were arranged with care on the rack, their vibrant colors bringing a splash of brightness to the room. They moved slowly and silently, not out of a lack of conversation—there were so many thoughts to share—but because words felt unnecessary in this quiet moment. The ease of their companionship filled the air, a comforting presence that needed no embellishment.

As Beck refolded a blanket, he glanced up. "You ready for this?"

Graham looked toward the guest room, where Naomi would stay after the wedding. "I don't think anyone's ever ready to say goodbye to forever."

Beck placed a hand on his brother's shoulder. "Then say yes to right now."

And in that space, warm and sacred, they still

found solace. The soft glow of the flickering candles cast gentle shadows on the walls, illuminating their faces with a golden hue. The air was infused with the faint scent of blooming jasmine, wrapping around them like a comforting embrace. At that moment, surrounded by the tranquility of the universe, they shared whispers and laughter, their hearts intertwined in a bond that transcended time. They truly understood what it meant to be alive and connected in this sanctuary of peace.

Chapter Sixteen: One Glorious Night

The Seacrest Inn welcomed Jennifer Jameson with a profound sense of peace that she hadn't realized she desperately needed. Room 204, infused with the subtle fragrance of lavender and the refreshing scent of salt air, enveloped her in a soothing embrace. Pale blue walls, reminiscent of a clear summer sky, were accented by elegant white crown molding, creating an atmosphere that felt both clean and comforting. The queen bed, dressed in a crisp white duvet that felt luxurious to the touch, promised restful nights. At the foot of the bed, a navy throw blanket, neatly folded, added a touch of warmth and homeliness.

A sturdy wooden desk, polished to a shine, featured a delicate blue-glass lamp that cast a gentle glow, inviting her to unwind with a book or journal. The large window framed a stunning view of the ocean, where waves danced playfully under the sun, while two cushioned armchairs, upholstered in soft fabric, offered a cozy spot to sit and gaze at the horizon. The sliding glass doors opened onto a private balcony, where the sound of the surf mingled with the whispers of a light breeze, creating a tranquil retreat that felt like her own sanctuary.

Jennifer pushed open the weathered wooden doors and stepped outside, allowing the salty ocean breeze to caress her cheeks. The Atlantic Ocean unfurled before her, shimmering in a tapestry of silver and soft gray-blue, with the early morning sun casting a gentle glow across the water's surface. Seagulls cawed overhead, their silhouettes dancing against the pastel sky. For a brief moment, she stood in serene silence, her eyes closed, fully absorbed in the rhythmic sound of the waves crashing against the rocky shoreline. Each swell brought with it a whisper of the sea's mysteries, inviting her to embrace the tranquility of the moment.

She sat on the edge of the bed, a soft quilt draping around her legs, as the gentle afternoon sunlight filtered through the sheer curtains. With a slight sigh, she picked up her phone and began to text her sons, her fingers gliding over the screen as she crafted each message with care. The faint sound of her boys playing outside drifted through the window, a reminder of the joyful chaos that filled her home.

Jennifer texted her sons, *"I just checked in. It's beautiful. Where should I meet you boys?"*

Within a matter of minutes, Beck swiftly responded with a concise yet inviting message: *"Let's meet for dinner at The Salty Lantern, a cozy seafood restaurant by the waterfront. How does 5:30 PM sound?"*

The Salty Lantern – Steak and Seafood was a hidden gem nestled along a charming historic brick street, just a short stroll from the vibrant promenade. With its weathered driftwood siding and warm, inviting facade, the restaurant exuded a rustic elegance reminiscent of seaside retreats. Flickering lanterns hung from the eaves, casting a gentle glow that danced along the pathway, while wide windows were swung open to invite the refreshing sea breeze, blending the indoor and outdoor spaces seamlessly.

Inside, the atmosphere was enhanced by the smooth sounds of a live saxophonist, filling the air with soft jazz that set a relaxed and sophisticated tone. The walls were adorned with an eclectic collection of nautical charts and vintage ship wheels, each telling a story of maritime adventure, while the subtle scent of grilled seafood and aged steak wafted through the space, enticing guests as they settled into plush, cozy seating. The warm, ambient lighting created an intimate setting that made every meal feel special, making The Salty Lantern a perfect destination for both casual diners and romantic evenings by the sea.

Jennifer arrived first and was seated near the large front window where the golden light of late afternoon spilled across the white linen tablecloth. The scent of grilled lemon, garlic butter, and herbed seafood drifted through the air. She looked around the space—couples laughing, glasses clinking, waitstaff moving efficiently—and felt a pang of something warm and sad.

The rest of the family arrived together, creating a comforting sense of unity as they approached. Naomi walked slowly, her frail form supported gently by Graham's sturdy arm. Each step was careful but steady, a testament to her determination. The soft fabric of her pale blue cardigan mirrored the serene hue of the sea just beyond the large glass windows as if she carried a piece of the ocean's calm within her. Behind them, Beck followed quietly, his expression contemplative, while Ruth and Thomas strolled closely together, their fingers entwined in a silent promise of support and love. The scene was one of warmth, underscored by the gentle lapping of waves in the distance. Jennifer stood to greet them.

"There's my girl," she whispered as she hugged Naomi tightly.

Naomi smiled. "You still know how to make an entrance."

"I learned from you."

They all laughed heartily, a warm and infectious sound that filled the cozy restaurant as they settled into their plush, upholstered seats at the oak table. The gentle hum of conversation and clinking of silverware around them created a lively backdrop.

Just then, their server approached with a welcoming smile, balancing a tray of steaming appetizers in one hand and a notepad in the other, ready to take their orders.

"I'm Camille," she said, a tall woman with warm auburn curls and a calm, confident presence. "It's a beautiful night for seafood and good company."

"We've got plenty of both," Thomas said.

Camille took their drink orders:
- Jennifer ordered a crisp glass of chardonnay
- Ruth requested a sparkling elderflower soda
- Naomi asked for iced tea with lemon
- Thomas chose a blackberry lemonade
- Beck opted for ginger ale with lime
- Graham asked for a Cape May IPA

"You've all got great taste," Camille said. "I'll be right back with these."

When she returned, they placed their dinner orders:

Naomi chose seared scallops with lemon risotto and grilled asparagus, her eyes drifting to Graham with a soft smile. Graham selected a medium rare ribeye with a loaded baked potato and charred green beans. Beck surprised them by going for mahi mahi tacos with mango slaw and sweet potato fries. Jennifer ordered the garlic butter lobster tail, roasted red potatoes, and broccolini. Ruth opted for crab-stuffed flounder with wild rice and cucumber salad.

Thomas grinned and said, "Surf and turf. Let's not pretend we didn't know."

Camille gave them a knowing smile. "You're in for a perfect meal."

The table lit up with stories, soft laughter, and shared memories. The conversation turned nostalgic as golden sunlight deepened outside, casting long shadows across the table.

"Remember that boardwalk summer?" Naomi asked. "Beck spent an embarrassing amount trying to win me a shark."

"Twenty bucks," Beck muttered. "Rigged game."

"I warned him," Jennifer added, sipping her wine.

"And I was the one who had to go back and apologize to the carny," Thomas laughed.

Dinner arrived in steaming, fragrant plates, and the room quieted in awe.

Naomi took her first bite and exhaled. "This... tastes like home."

Jennifer smiled. "It tastes like memory."

Later, as they each had a slice of key lime pie, Naomi leaned into Graham's shoulder.

"I want to hold this night forever."

He pressed his lips to her hair. "We already are."

As evening settled over Congress Hall Lawn, the vibrant atmosphere came alive with a kaleidoscope of colors and the cheerful sounds of laughter and chatter. Vendors enthusiastically offered their wares, with the enticing aroma of roasted corn wafting through the air, mingling with the refreshing scent of lemonade slushies served icy cold in clear plastic cups. Nearby, artisans skillfully crafted and displayed handmade shell jewelry that glimmered under the soft glow of decorative lights strung carefully between lusciously leafy trees. As twilight deepened, the twinkling lights began to cast a magical shimmer, creating an enchanting ambiance that invited visitors to linger and soak in the joyous spirit of the evening.

Naomi and Graham found a quiet spot on a large quilt they'd brought. She sat carefully, stretching her legs, and he sat beside her, arm looped around her waist. Ruth and Thomas settled nearby in folding chairs. Jennifer perched elegantly on a bench behind them, watching everything with discerning eyes.

Beck wandered through the sun-dappled park, the gentle rustle of leaves filling the air around him. His gaze eventually landed on Willow, who sat nestled under a sprawling oak tree, its branches casting playful shadows on the ground. She cradled a cold soda in her hand, the condensation glistening in the warm afternoon light. With a smile, Beck made his way over to her, feeling a sense of ease wash over him as he approached this quiet moment amidst the lively sounds of the park.

"You good?" she asked.

"Getting there," he said, eyes on Graham and Naomi.

"They look like a painting," Willow whispered. "Like something permanent."

Beck remained silent, his eyes fixed on the scene unfolding before him. The sun cast a warm glow on the surroundings, illuminating the subtle tension in the air as he absorbed every detail, from the rustling leaves to the faint sounds of laughter in the distance. He stood still, a thoughtful expression etched on his face, taking in both the beauty and the complexity of the moment.

The first firework exploded at precisely 9:30 PM, filling the night sky with a brilliant burst of crimson red that radiated outward like a blooming flower. Moments later, cascading silver stars followed, twinkling and sizzling as they arced gracefully through the darkness, leaving shimmering trails that seemed to dance in the cool evening air. The distant sound of oohs and aahs from the crowd underscored the magic of the moment, making it feel as though the very stars had come alive for a breathtaking display.

Naomi's eyes widened. "I forgot how loud they are."

"Still beautiful," Graham said. "Still loud."

She leaned into him, the warmth of her cheek pressed against his stubbled jaw. The next explosion erupted overhead, filling the night sky with brilliant gold sparks, casting a dazzling glow across her features and making her emerald eyes shimmer like precious gems. Naomi turned to him, her breath catching in her throat, and at that perfect moment—timed flawlessly with a thunderous burst of light—Graham leaned in and kissed her. It was slow, each second stretching out like an eternity; steady, like a promise waiting to be fulfilled; and sure, filled with an unspoken assurance that this moment was theirs alone, unshakeable amidst the chaos around them.

A few feet away, Beck quietly pulled out his phone, his heartbeat harmonizing with the distant crackle of fireworks. He refrained from using the flash, wanting to preserve the intimacy of the moment. Just one photo. In that fleeting second, he captured them in silhouette against the vibrant bursts of color—Naomi's delicate hand tenderly resting on Graham's cheek, their faces cast in soft shadows, illuminated by the exploding lights behind them. The fireworks created a dazzling frame that turned the scene into a celestial halo; each sparks mirroring the warmth of their connection. It was the kind of image that felt timeless, a moment so pure that not even the relentless march of time could steal its essence.

"I love you," Naomi whispered as their foreheads touched.

"I'll love you long after the sky quiets," Graham replied.

A final firework bloomed above them—shimmering pink, gold, then white—and Naomi closed her eyes, tears clinging to her lashes.

Behind them, Jennifer dabbed her eyes.

"They're writing their forever," Ruth said quietly.

Thomas squeezed her hand. "And we're lucky to witness it."

At home, Graham gently assisted Naomi in changing into her soft, flannel pajamas, the fabric warm against her skin. Once dressed, she sank into the plush cushions of the couch, the familiar scent of lavender from her favorite blanket wrapping around her like a comforting embrace. Her body, fatigued from the day's demands, settled into the cozy nook, yet her cheeks held a healthy, radiant glow. As she nestled deeper under the blanket's weight, a peaceful sigh escaped her lips, signaling her contentment in this serene moment.

Inside the cozy room, dimly lit by the soft glow of a nearby lamp, Naomi nestled into Graham's warm embrace, her head resting gently against his chest. Her eyes, heavy with sleep, fluttered half-closed as she sought comfort in the rhythmic beat of his heart. The faint scent of his cologne mingled with the peaceful atmosphere, enveloping them in a tranquil cocoon of intimacy and security.

"That was perfect," she murmured.

He kissed her forehead. "You were perfect."

Chapter Seventeen: The Promise

The sun rose gently over Cape May, its golden rays spilling across the quaint Victorian rooftops and stretching long shadows onto the narrow cobblestone streets below. At Naomi's house, a cozy cottage with pastel-colored shutters and blooming window boxes, the air was still, infused with the sweet scent of saltwater and blooming honeysuckle. The morning held its breath as if even time paused, aware of the significance of this day, wrapping the town in a tranquil hush. A few chirping sparrows flitted about, their soft melodies adding to the serene atmosphere, while the horizon gradually brightened, heralding the promise of a beautiful day ahead.

Naomi sat at the weathered porch table, a soft, light robe cinched around her, its fabric whispering against her skin. In her hands, she cradled a steaming cup of fragrant peppermint tea, the aromatic steam curling up toward her face, bringing a sense of warmth and comfort. Her gaze wandered over the vibrant green treetops that framed the horizon, where the deep blue of the sea glimmered under the sunlight like a vast sapphire. A gentle breeze tousled her hair, sending a few loose strands dancing around her face as she let out a soft sigh, embracing the tranquility that enveloped her. The only sounds were the distant calls of seabirds and the rhythmic lapping of waves against the shore, blending into the serene atmosphere of the moment.

Willow sat cross-legged on the cozy, worn sofa, her fingers deftly peeling a bright orange clementine, the sweet citrus scent filling the air. She had arrived early, the morning light streaming through the window, casting a warm glow on the table where she had carefully arranged an assortment of flaky pastries and plump, juicy blueberries she had sourced from the local market that vibrant Saturday morning. The delicate pastries, still warm from the oven, glistened with a hint of sugar, while the blueberries sparkled like tiny jewels, inviting and fresh.

"You slept?" Willow asked softly.

"Some," Naomi replied. "Not much. But I don't think I needed much."

As soon as Jennifer stepped into the kitchen, the rich aroma of freshly brewed coffee began to fill the air, mingling with the warmth of the sun filtering through the window. The scent wafted out into the hall, inviting and comforting. Ruth, ever-bustling, moved with quiet purpose among the countertops, her hands expertly chopping vegetables for breakfast, a hint of flour dusting her apron.

Chloe, Naomi's younger cousin, emerged from the guest room. Her shoulder-length chestnut hair was still tousled and slightly sleep-rumpled, hinting at the late night of laughter and stories shared. Stretching her arms overhead, she blinked sleepily against the morning light, a faint smile forming as the familiar scents of home wrapped around her.

"Good morning," she said, offering a small wave. "I can help with anything."

Naomi smiled. "Just be here. That's more than

enough."

Across town, Graham's home—a charming single-story gray house with white trim and a black front door—was beginning to stir. In the kitchen, Beck poured black coffee into mismatched mugs while Miles nervously adjusted his collar in the hallway mirror.

"I think I tied this wrong."

"You're not wearing a tie," Beck said dryly, handing him a cinnamon roll.

Graham stood on the back deck, barefoot on the cool wooden planks, his hands tucked into the pockets of his faded jeans. He gazed out at the backyard, where the late morning sun bathed the lush green grass in a golden hue. The air was fresh with the scent of blooming flowers, and the distant sound of birds chirping filled the serene atmosphere. A gentle breeze rustled the leaves of the nearby trees, creating a soothing symphony that complemented the warm embrace of sunlight on his skin.

Thomas joined him with two mugs, handing one over. "You ready?"

"I think I've been ready for years," Graham said. "But today... it feels heavier. In a good way."

Thomas placed a hand on his shoulder. "You make her feel safe. Loved. Seen. That's what matters most."

Inside, Miles glanced again at the group photo on Graham's mantel—his eyes landing on Naomi. "She's incredible."

Beck followed his gaze. "So's her cousin."

Miles raised a brow. "You noticed too?"

Beck laughed. "She smiled at you yesterday. I thought you were going to pass out."

Miles flushed. "She smiled like... she knew something I didn't."

As mid-morning sunlight streamed through her window, a subtle shift in energy filled the air—there was an unmistakable sense of movement and purpose beyond the stillness of the early hours. Naomi returned to her cozy room, the familiar scent of aged wood and ink enveloping her as she approached her writing desk, a well-loved piece adorned with scattered notes and the occasional ink stain. Before her, a small folded paper lay like a delicate secret—her vow, her promise, waiting to be unveiled. She inhaled deeply, the quiet stillness grounding her as she reached for her favorite fountain pen, its silver nib glinting in the light. With a gentle motion, she uncapped the pen and poised it over the paper, ready to breathe life into her thoughts. She began to write, each stroke of the pen an expression of her hopes and determination.

Sitting on the weathered wooden planks of the back porch at Graham's house, he took a moment to savor the tranquility that surrounded him. The soft rustling of leaves danced with the gentle breeze while the distant sound of birds chirping filled the air. With a notebook open on his lap, he wrote intently, each stroke of the pen steady and purposeful, as he immersed himself in the quietude of the moment. The fading afternoon light bathed the space in a warm golden glow, creating a serene backdrop for his thoughts to flow freely.

Early that afternoon, the soft chime of the doorbell announced Pastor Eli Whitcomb's arrival. With a warm smile, he greeted Ruth and Jennifer at the door, his kind eyes reflecting genuine concern. After exchanging pleasantries, he made his way to Naomi's room, the faint scent of lavender from the hallway mingling with the quiet atmosphere.

Inside, he found Naomi seated in a pale blue robe that complemented the soft light streaming through the window. Her hands were delicately folded in her lap, the subtle tremor of her fingers betraying the calm she tried to project. She looked up at him, her eyes a mix of gratitude and vulnerability, ready to share whatever lay heavy on her heart.

"Naomi," he said, taking a seat beside her. "It's an honor to stand with you today. But first, I want to speak a blessing over you."

He opened his Bible and read softly:

"Love is patient, love is kind. It does not envy, it does not boast... It bears all things, believes all things, hopes all things, endures all things. Love never fails." – 1 Corinthians 13

Tears welled in Naomi's eyes as Pastor Whitcomb placed a hand on her shoulder and prayed.

Later, as the sun began to set, casting a warm golden hue over the landscape, Graham sat on the weathered wooden porch of his home. The air was filled with the scent of blooming jasmine, and the sounds of evening crickets began to fill the silence. Pastor Whitcomb approached; his footsteps were soft on the creaking boards. Without hesitation, he took a seat beside Graham, his worn Bible resting on his lap. After a brief moment of contemplation, he opened it and read aloud from Romans 12:12, the words flowing with conviction:

"Be joyful in hope, patient in affliction, faithful in prayer."

The two men sat quietly for a moment, allowing the message to resonate between them as they contemplated its significance in their lives.

"Rejoice in hope, be patient in tribulation, be

constant in prayer."

He closed the worn, leather-bound Bible, the scent of aged paper lingering in the air, and then turned his gaze toward Graham, locking eyes with a fierce intensity that spoke volumes.

"You're marrying more than a woman today. You're marrying her story. Her strength. Her soul."

Graham nodded, his throat tight with unspoken emotion, a lump rising that made it difficult for him to articulate his thoughts. The weight of the moment pressed down on him, each breath feeling heavy as he fought to contain the surge of feelings welling up inside.

As the day stretched toward evening, anticipation filled the air, and the final preparations unfolded with a sense of urgency. Naomi's light blue sundress, the soft and flowing fabric hung gracefully from the closet door, catching the warm glow of the evening light. Each delicate stitch of the dress whispered promises of joy and new beginnings.

Her bouquet—a stunning arrangement of five vibrant blue roses and three pristine white ones, all elegantly intertwined with wispy baby's breath—sat atop the dresser, a symbol of love and celebration. The stems were artfully wrapped in a luxurious white ribbon that added a touch of elegance.

Ruth, bustling around the room with a knowing smile, had thoughtfully delivered the bouquet and made sure the rings were safely tucked away in their velvet-lined box, nestled securely among silk cushions. Her careful attention to detail ensured that everything was perfect for the momentous occasion ahead.

In the bedroom, Willow helped Naomi step into her dress, handling the fabric with care. The breeze through the open window carried the scent of salt and jasmine.

Chloe stood behind Naomi, her fingers deftly curling and pinning Naomi's dark, silken hair into soft, romantic waves that cascaded gently down her back. With a keen eye for detail, she skillfully wove in delicate sprigs of tiny white flowers, their petals reminiscent of fresh snowfall, creating a charming contrast against the deep richness of the hair. The sweet, subtle fragrance of the blossoms filled the air, adding an enchanting touch to the intimate scene as Chloe ensured every curl and flower was perfectly placed, transforming Naomi into a vision of beauty.

"You're glowing," Chloe whispered.

"I feel it," Naomi said, smiling. "Like my body remembers how to be whole, just for today."

Jennifer joined them, dabbing a brush across Naomi's cheeks with a hint of natural blush, soft mascara on her lashes, and a pale shimmer on her lips. "Just a touch of grace," she said.

As the door creaked open, Layla stepped into the room, her violin case swinging slightly at her side. The polished wood gleamed under the soft light, hinting at the craftsmanship within. With a playful grin, she looked around at her friends gathered in anticipation. "Ready when you are," she said, her voice melodic and warm. "Don't cry yet—I haven't even started playing," she added teasingly, her eyes sparkling with excitement. The air was thick with anticipation, the faint scent of lingering varnish and hardwood filling the space, creating a perfect backdrop for the music about to unfold.

The golden beach shimmered under the warm sunlight, with grains of fine sand that felt soft and warm beneath my feet. The sound of gentle waves lapping against the shore created a soothing melody, while seagulls danced in the clear blue sky above. In the distance, vibrant shells nestled among the dunes added splashes of color to the idyllic scene, making it a picture-perfect coastal paradise.

The guests sat on wooden benches nestled into the sand, the Atlantic whispering in the distance. A white arch wrapped in blue and white roses stood facing the sea. Fairy lights were strung loosely between the dunes, catching the soft light of early evening.

Layla stood to the side, violin tucked under her chin. As Naomi appeared at the edge of the boardwalk, she began to play—slow, aching notes of "Hallelujah."

Naomi walked barefoot, Thomas at her side, her dress catching the breeze. When they reached the arch, Thomas pressed a kiss to Naomi's cheek and then turned to sit beside Ruth.

Graham's breath hitched as he took Naomi's hand. "You're more beautiful than the first day I met you."

Naomi smiled. "You remembered."

Pastor Whitcomb welcomed everyone to the gathering with his signature warmth and brevity, his voice resonating with sincerity as he gestured toward the congregation. He made eye contact with several attendees, creating a sense of connection, before briefly outlining the day's schedule and emphasizing the importance of community and open dialogue.

He spoke of a profound love that transcends the boundaries of time, a love that remains unwavering even as seasons change. He described the grace that is deliberately chosen each day, a conscious decision to nurture and cherish one another in both joy and hardship. He emphasized the courage it takes to commit fully, knowing that the future is shrouded in uncertainty, yet embracing that unpredictability as an inherent part of their journey together.

Naomi's voice trembled as she read her vows:

"You are my harbor, my healing, my home. If I have just one more season, I want to spend it wrapped in your love."

Graham's voice cracked as he replied:

"You are the piece of me I didn't know was missing. And I vow to be your peace, your steady ground, your forever—even if forever is shorter than I wish."

As they stood barefoot on the sun-warmed sand, they exchanged exquisite rings, each glinting in the soft glow of the setting sun. With the rhythmic sound of waves breaking gently behind them, they leaned in, their hearts racing, and shared a tender kiss, a moment that felt suspended in time, surrounded by the salty breeze and the scent of the ocean.

And the crowd—small, intimate, full of love—rose to their feet, clapping and weeping.

The reception took place in Naomi's picturesque backyard, which was gently illuminated by twinkling string lights that hung gracefully from the branches of the oak trees overhead. The warm glow created an enchanting atmosphere as evening fell. A small buffet spread out enticingly, featuring delicately crafted chicken salad croissants nestled on a rustic wooden platter, vibrant fresh fruit skewers bursting with color, an assortment of cheese trays displaying a variety of artisanal cheeses paired with savory crackers, and golden-brown mini quiches filled with spinach and cheese.

Nearby, a beautifully arranged table showcased a

stunning two-tier wedding cake adorned with pressed edible flowers that elegantly decorated the frosted surface, perfectly reflecting the garden theme. Alongside the cake, a large bowl of sparkling fruit punch shimmered in the light, inviting guests to scoop a refreshing glass full of its fruity goodness. The overall scene radiated warmth and joy, capturing the essence of a perfect celebration.
A soft instrumental playlist played in the background as Naomi and Graham shared their first dance in the grass: barefoot, slow, and close.

Jennifer raised her glass first for the toast.

"To the love we hope to find, and the love we're lucky enough to hold. To Graham and Naomi—may every moment you have together echo in all of us."

Naomi squeezed Graham's hand as everyone cheered.

Beck and Willow stood quietly at the edge of the lawn. She nudged him gently. "You look like you believe in love again."

"I do," he said. "At least in theirs."

Miles sat on the weathered porch stairs, the wood creaking softly beneath him, while Chloe settled in next to him. The late afternoon sun cast a warm golden glow over the scene, illuminating the vibrant colors of her floral dress, which danced gently in the breeze and brushed against his arm. The sweet scent of blooming jasmine wafted through the air, mingling with the faint sound of birds chirping in the distance, creating a serene atmosphere that wrapped around them like a comforting blanket.

"Thanks for sitting with me," he said.

Chloe smiled. "Thanks for noticing. "He glanced toward the couple. "I think this… changed me."

"Me too," she whispered.

Later that night, at Graham's and Naomi's cozy home, a warm glow spilled from the windows, casting soft golden light onto the porch where Graham and Naomi stood, enveloped in a gentle embrace of cool evening air. Graham leaned against the wooden railing, gazing thoughtfully into the distance, while Naomi, wrapped in a light cardigan, pulled her hair back, revealing a serene smile as she took in the moment with him.

"Did it feel like enough?" he asked.

Naomi leaned her head on his shoulder.

"It felt like forever."

Chapter Eighteen: The List

The next day, Naomi stirred just before the first rays of dawn crept through the heavy curtains, casting a soft glow across the room. The air still held the tranquil hush of night, thick with the scent of lavender from the sachets tucked into the corners. For a fleeting moment, she thought she was lost in a dream—wrapped snugly in fluffy blankets that enveloped her like a gentle cocoon. The warmth beside her radiated a comforting heat, and she could hear the steady rhythm of Graham's breathing, deep and even, filling the quiet space with a serene intimacy.

She turned her head slowly, allowing her gaze to linger on him—peaceful in the soft glow of the evening light, his dark lashes casting faint shadows over his smooth cheeks. A warmth filled her heart as it swelled with affection. She watched him for a few precious seconds, committing to memory the gentle rhythm of his chest rising and falling, a steady cadence that seemed to sync with her breath. The moment's serenity enveloped her, every detail etched in her mind—the slight crinkle at the corners of his eyes, the way a stray lock of hair fell across his forehead, and the comfortable silence surrounding them.

Then she leaned closer, pressed her lips to his shoulder, and whispered, "Graham... wake up."

He shifted slightly on the plush couch, the soft

fabric cradling his frame. A faint smile danced across his lips as he blinked slowly, hinting at the remnants of a pleasant dream. Gradually, his eyes fluttered open, revealing a deep, thoughtful gaze that took a moment to focus on the world around him fully.

"What is it?" he murmured, his voice thick with sleep.

"The sunrise," she whispered. "Will you watch it with me?"

He sat up slowly, rubbing his eyes. "Absolutely."

They wrapped themselves in one of the soft, knit blankets from the couch, its fibers warm against their skin, and stepped outside barefoot onto the wooden porch. The early morning air was cool and damp, carrying the fresh scent of dew-kissed grass and the faint, earthy aroma of fallen leaves. The porch boards felt cold and slightly rough beneath their feet, sending a shiver up their spines. Naomi settled onto the top step, her legs tucked beneath her, while Graham joined her, shifting closer. She nestled against him, seeking the warmth radiating from his body, the blanket a cozy cocoon around them. Together, they watched the soft light of dawn break across the horizon, painting the sky in pale pink and lavender hues, as the world slowly awakened around them.

Before them, the world began to glow with warm, golden light, casting long shadows that danced across the lush green landscape. As the sun dipped below the horizon, hues of orange and pink painted the sky while the trees shimmered with the soft luminescence of fireflies emerging from their hiding places. The air buzzed with anticipation, charged with the scent of blooming wildflowers and the gentle rustle of leaves as if nature was awakening to twilight's magic.

"I've always loved how quiet the world is before it wakes," she said.

Graham took her hand. "It's like it's holding its breath. Just for us."

Naomi smiled. "It's on my list, you know. My bucket list."

He turned toward her. "Watching the sunrise?"

She nodded. "With you."

Graham didn't speak right away. Instead, he squeezed her hand tightly, feeling the warmth of her palm against his. He gazed at the horizon as the deep hues of night gradually gave way to the soft pastels of dawn. Wisps of lavender and pink melted into the deep blue of the fading night sky, and the first light of day flickered on the edges of the clouds, transforming the world around them. The air was crisp and cool, filled with the gentle rustle of leaves and the distant chirping of birds waking for the day. Time seemed to stand still as they shared this moment, a silent promise lingering between them as the stars slowly dimmed.

By midmorning, the soft rays of sunlight filtered through the sheer curtains, casting a warm glow in the bedroom where Naomi had curled up under the cozy quilt for a short nap. The room was filled with the gentle hum of the outside world, lulling her deeper into sleep. Meanwhile, Graham quietly tiptoed out of the room, making sure not to disturb her peace. Almost an hour later, he returned with a sense of anticipation, holding a charming white bakery box from Ever After Bakery. It was elegantly tied with a pale yellow ribbon that fluttered slightly with his movement, hinting at the delightful treats nestled inside. The sweet aroma wafting from the box promised a delightful surprise, one that he hoped would bring a smile to Naomi's face when she awoke.

He found Naomi on the weathered wooden porch again, her figure cocooned in a soft, oversized cardigan that was a faded shade of lavender. The afternoon sun cast a warm glow around her as she sat cross-legged in a wicker chair, her brow slightly furrowed in concentration as she scribbled thoughts and observations into her well-worn journal. The gentle breeze carried the scent of blooming jasmine from the garden, creating a serene backdrop to her quiet moment of reflection.

"For you," he said, placing the box gently on her lap.

Naomi looked down at the delicate box in her hands, her brow furrowed in confusion. With hesitant fingers, she lifted the lid, revealing a small, round lemon cake nestled inside. The cake was expertly baked, its golden hue glistening under the soft light. It was generously covered in a fluffy layer of whipped frosting that appeared almost cloud-like, and it was adorned with vibrant candied lemon zest that shimmered invitingly. Scattered atop were delicate edible petals, their colors adding a touch of elegance to the already inviting dessert. Naomi's hand instinctively moved to cover her mouth as she gasped in surprise, a sense of delight washing over her at the unexpected treat before her.

"You remembered," she whispered.

Graham sat beside her. "You used to sneak slices when we were teenagers. I just thought it might bring back something sweet."

Tears filled her eyes. "It was on my list."

Graham blinked. "Wait—seriously?"

She laughed through the emotion. "I didn't expect it, but... yes. That cake. From this place."

He shook his head, smiling. "Well, now I'm going to read that list."

Naomi hesitated for a moment, her brow furrowing as she contemplated the significance of the journal. With a determined breath, she turned it toward him, the worn leather cover creaking softly. As she meticulously flipped through the pages, the scent of aged paper filled the air, mingling with the faint aroma of lavender from a pressed flower that had been tucked away. She paused occasionally to examine the entries—some were meticulously penned in elegant cursive, while others had faded and blurred with time, their clarity diminishing like distant memories. There were also fresh, inked passages intertwined among them, evidence of recent thoughts and feelings spilling out, eager to be documented.

— Watch the sunrise
— Lemon cake from Ever After
— A boat ride one more time
— Watch the sunset
— Leave a note at the Turning Page
— Dance in the rain
— Write letters

Graham carefully read each item on the list, his brow furrowed in concentration as if he feared that his eyes might skip over something precious and irreplaceable. Each word seemed to carry a weight of significance that he didn't want to overlook. As he absorbed the details, a wave of emotion washed over him, and he instinctively reached out, wrapping his arms around her in a gentle embrace, seeking both comfort and connection in that moment. The warmth of their shared presence felt like a quiet promise, a sanctuary amidst the chaos of life.

"We're doing it," he said. "We're living it."

Naomi rested her head against his chest. "We are."

That afternoon, a gentle breeze swept across the marina, carrying with it the refreshing scent of saltwater and sun-kissed wood. The sky overhead was a brilliant azure, dotted with only a few fluffy white clouds lazily drifting by, while the water below shimmered like a thousand diamonds under the warm embrace of the summer sun.

Naomi stood at the edge of the dock, her wide-brimmed straw hat protecting her from the sun's rays, casting a soft shadow across her face. She wore a delicate pale blue sundress that danced around her knees in the light breeze, and a sea-glass pendant—a muted green hue—rested just over her heart, a memento from her last seaside adventure.

Graham, tall and tanned, extended his hand to help her board the sailboat, the weathered wooden deck creaking slightly under their weight. The boat, with its crisp white sails fluttering eagerly against the backdrop of blue, seemed to beckon them into the open waters. Following Naomi, Willow, with her tousled hair blowing in the wind, climbed aboard, her laughter mingling with the sound of gently lapping waves. Next came Chloe, her enthusiasm palpable, as she practically skipped up the gangway, closely followed by Beck, who carried a cooler filled with snacks, and Miles, who was busy adjusting his sunglasses in preparation for an afternoon of fun on the water.

It wasn't extravagant—just a half-day rental arranged by Layla, who'd insisted it was "exactly the kind of memory they needed."

Naomi stood at the bow, arms out for a moment, the wind catching her hair. She turned to Graham, laughing softly. "I feel seventeen again."

Beck lifted his camera, its lens catching the warm, golden light of the late afternoon sun, and began capturing quiet, candid photos. He focused on the way the wind tousled Naomi's hair, creating a halo of sun-kissed strands around her face. Chloe and Miles sat side by side, their laughter ringing out like music as they exchanged playful glances, their eyes sparkling with joy. Meanwhile, Graham was lost in thought, his gaze fixed on Naomi with a soft, infinite love that spoke volumes without a single word. Nearby, Willow emerged from the cooler, balancing a tray of refreshing drinks, each one glistening with condensation. She passed the drinks around, the vibrant colors of the beverages contrasting beautifully with the rich greens of the surrounding grass. As she settled down on the grassy edge, with her feet dangling carefree over the side, the scene painted a perfect picture of a warm, lazy day spent together, full of laughter and unspoken connections.

"Did I tell you about the first time I went sailing?" Naomi said, grinning.

"You hated it," Willow replied. "Said the boat moved like a drunk uncle."

Everyone laughed.

They talked for hours, their conversation flowing effortlessly—reminiscing about childhood adventures, debating the quirks of adulthood, and diving deep into the intricacies of their hopes and dreams. Naomi held Graham's hand tenderly, brushing her thumb over his knuckles as she planted soft kisses on them mid-sentence, her gaze warm and unwavering. Chloe leaned into Miles, feeling the comforting warmth of his presence, their shoulders brushing lightly, creating a shared cocoon of intimacy amidst the night. Meanwhile, Beck captured every moment with quiet reverence, his camera clicking softly, preserving their laughter and whispered secrets against the backdrop of a fading sunset.

But the joy shifted quickly.

As they docked, Naomi gripped the rail and paled.

"Naomi?" Graham asked.

Without warning, she pivoted on the wooden deck and leaned over the side of the boat, the salty spray of the ocean mixing with the contents of her stomach. Her hands trembled uncontrollably, the nervous energy radiating from her as the waves lapped against the hull. Everyone froze, stunned into silence at the sudden shift in the atmosphere. Beck, quickly realizing the gravity of the situation, tucked his phone into his pocket, its screen darkening in contrast to the scene unfolding before them. Chloe's breath caught in her throat, unsure whether to rush to her friend or remain paralyzed by shock. An oppressive silence enveloped the group, each member absorbing the weight of unspoken concerns. Naomi wiped her mouth with the back of her hand, her face pale yet displaying an unexpected calmness. When she turned back to them, her eyes were glassy, betraying the turmoil within her, but she carried herself with a serene acceptance as if she had already reconciled with whatever was causing her distress.

"It's okay," she said softly. "It's part of it. Don't be afraid of it... I'm not."

Chloe's face crumpled in anguish, her delicate features twisted with sorrow as she covered her mouth with trembling fingers, tears spilling down her cheeks like a sudden rain. Miles, sensing her pain, reached out instinctively and wrapped a comforting arm around her shoulders, pulling her close to him as if to shield her from the weight of the world. In the soft glow of the fading light, their surroundings fell away, and no one attempted to interrupt the moment. They stood together in the stillness, enveloped in an unspoken understanding, letting the raw emotion hang in the air, a silent acknowledgment of their shared burden.

Naomi leaned against Graham, whispering, "Let's go home."

That evening, the golden hour bathed the world in a warm, honeyed glow as Graham and Beck carefully maneuvered the last of Naomi's boxes into Graham's cozy house. The crisp scent of freshly cut grass wafted through the air, mingling with the distant sound of laughter from children playing outside. Inside the boxes were familiar treasures: well-loved books with dog-eared pages, a soft, intricately knit shawl that had once belonged to her grandmother, her cherished sketchpads filled with delicate pencil drawings, and the sea-glass jar she'd always kept on her windowsill, glistening with memories of sun and surf.

Naomi rested on the plush, inviting couch, her eyes closed but her mind acutely aware, listening to the gentle thud of boxes being set down and the hushed conversations that punctuated the focused movements around her. The living room, adorned with softly patterned cushions and a handwoven rug, felt welcoming and safe, a place she now proudly called home. Her journal lay open on her lap, its well-worn pages filled with thoughts and dreams. With a sigh, she picked up her favorite pen—a smooth, sparkling fountain pen gifted by her late mother—and began to write, capturing the moment and the emotions swirling within her.

"Today, I was reminded that even fading stars light the sky before they disappear. I watched the sunrise with the man I love, ate cake that tasted like a memory, and sailed across the water that has always known my name. I laughed. I cried. I was alive in every sense of the word. And yes... I was sick, too. But even that didn't take away the beauty. I don't know how many more days I'll have like this, but if this is what love looks like—unflinching, unshaken, still standing beside me—I'll go with peace in my bones. Tonight, I'm not afraid. I'm grateful."

She turned her gaze toward the window, drawn by the moon's silvery glow as it began its ascent into the night sky. The faint moonlight shimmer danced across the room, casting soft shadows on the walls. A gentle breeze rustled the curtains, carrying with it the crisp scent of the evening. A smile blossomed on her lips, warmth flooding her heart as the tranquil beauty of the moment enveloped her.

Chapter Ninteen: Slowing Time

By the middle of July, the air in Cape May had softened into a tender embrace. Summer's typical intensity gave way to a gentler ambiance, with breezes that danced like whispers through the leafy branches of the sycamores lining the streets. Once harsh and unyielding, the sunlight now bathed the Victorian houses in a warm, golden hue, casting long, intricate shadows on the cobblestone paths. That unique, tranquil quiet—the kind that settles around a place when the cicadas eventually hush, and the ocean waves lapping lazily against the shoreline—suggests the world understands it's time to pause and breathe.

Naomi lay curled up on the worn, dark leather couch beneath a soft, pale blue knit blanket that hugged her form snugly. Her breaths came slow and shallow, a rhythmic rise and fall that whispered of peaceful slumber. Her hands rested gently near her heart, fingers delicately curled inward as if cradling a cherished secret. Even in her dreams, there was an ethereal quality about her—a fragile paper lantern glowing softly from within, the faint light casting gentle shadows around the room, hinting at warmth and tranquility. The setting was quiet, punctuated only by the soft rustle of the blanket and the occasional distant sound of city life, creating a serene cocoon around her.

Graham sat nearby, his coffee growing cold in his

hands, the steam rising in thin tendrils that lingered in the air, as he watched her sleep. The sunlight filtered through the window, casting a gentle glow on her face, which seemed to hold a serene beauty even in slumber. She'd been sleeping more often now, drifting in and out like waves pulling back from the shore, the ebb and flow of her consciousness becoming a familiar rhythm. Every day, he noticed something new: the way her shoulders slumped a bit more under the weight of unseen burdens, how her appetite had dwindled, each meager bite a struggle; he recalled how she used to relish her meals, savoring each flavor like a cherished memory. Her voice had grown softer, like a whisper caught in the stillness of the afternoon, almost hesitant, as if she was afraid of breaking the fragile silence that surrounded them.

But her spirit? That was still so fiercely hers. It flickered like a candle in the wind, resilient and unwavering, lighting up the dim corners of her struggle. Even in her quiet moments, there was a spark—a determination that shone through her weary eyes, reminding him that despite everything, she still fought to hold onto who she was.

He set his steaming mug of coffee down on the small wooden table, the rich aroma lingering in the air. Kneeling beside her, he gently brushed a loose strand of chestnut hair away from her pale cheek, his fingers lingering for a moment against her soft skin. The warm glow of the afternoon sun filtered through the window, casting a golden light that illuminated her features, highlighting both the vulnerability and strength in her expression

"Naomi," he whispered, his voice warm and reverent.

She stirred, eyes fluttering open. "Mm... did I fall asleep again?"

"Just a little," he smiled. "You looked peaceful."

She reached for his hand and gave it a gentle squeeze. "I dreamed I was walking through a lemon grove. The sun was warm, and someone was laughing."

Graham kissed her cheek. "You must've heard me trying to sing earlier."

She chuckled softly. "That explains it."

As they strolled through the charming, cobbled streets of downtown Cape May, Chloe and Miles took their time, savoring the vibrant atmosphere around them. Chloe looked effortlessly elegant in a flowing white sundress, the fabric dancing lightly around her knees with each step. Her sun-kissed hair was pinned loosely at the back, soft tendrils framing her face. Beside her, Miles opted for a laid-back yet polished look, wearing well-fitted jeans paired with a classic navy polo that highlighted his relaxed demeanor.

The sun spilled warm light over the picturesque scene as they passed by a series of quaint shops, their storefronts adorned with colorful flower boxes brimming with blooms. The sweet aroma of freshly baked pastries wafted from a nearby bakery, where golden croissants and vibrant macarons tempted passersby. Hand in hand, Chloe and Miles exchanged smiles, indulging in the simple joy of being together in such a delightful setting.

"You know," Chloe said, "you're really into this older woman thing."

Miles grinned. "You're older by a year, Chloe."

She raised a brow. "A year and three months."

"Oh, well, in that case, I should be calling you ma'am."

She swatted his shoulder with a laugh. "Careful. I know where you sleep."

They paused in front of Ever After Bakery, captivated by the colorful display in the window. Sunlight danced off the glass, illuminating the delicate layers of rich lemon cakes topped with zesty frosting, while the sweet aroma of freshly baked cherry scones wafted through the air, hinting at their warm, flaky texture. Iced cookies shaped like starfish completed the scene, their vibrant pastel colors and intricate designs enticing passersby with a promise of delightful sweetness and a touch of whimsy.

Miles leaned closer. "We should bring something back for Naomi later. Cake, maybe?"

Chloe smiled. "You're always thinking about other people. It's one of the things I like about you."

He shrugged. "I learned from Graham and Beck. And from you."

Back at home, Naomi had taken a moment to freshen up, running a brush through her hair and splashing cool water on her face. Now, she sat upright on the edge of the couch, wrapped in a soft, knitted blanket that provided a sense of comfort against the chill in the air. The late afternoon sun streamed through the window, casting a warm glow across the living room when the doorbell rang, its chime echoing softly in the stillness.

Graham opened the door to reveal Cassidy Ward, the hospice nurse, standing on the porch with a navy supply case in hand. Dressed in navy scrubs, she exuded professionalism tempered with genuine warmth. Her smile was infectious, radiating compassion and a deep understanding that came from years of experience in her line of work. As she stepped onto the threshold, her eyes sparkled gently, reassuring Naomi and Graham that they were not alone in this challenging moment.

"Good morning," Cassidy said gently. "I brought the good stuff."

Naomi laughed lightly. "Fluids and electrolytes. Who knew they'd be the highlight of my week?"

Cassidy strolled into the living room, her canvas bag slung confidently over her shoulder. As she set down her belongings—a sleek laptop, a vibrant sketchbook, and an assortment of colorful pens—she took a moment to survey her surroundings. The warm afternoon light streamed through the large windows, casting soft shadows on the hardwood floor. With ease, she arranged her things on the rustic coffee table, absentmindedly fluffing the cozy throw pillows on the couch. The inviting scent of freshly brewed coffee lingered in the air, making her feel right at home as she settled into her creative space.

"How's your pain been today?" she asked.

"Better," Naomi said. "But I'm tired. All the time."

"That's normal," Cassidy replied softly. "We'll help with comfort where we can."

Graham sat close by, his fingers gently entwined with Naomi's as she lay in the hospital bed, the harsh fluorescent lights casting a pale glow over her face. Cassidy, the nurse, moved with practiced efficiency as she prepared the IV. The soft rustle of her scrubs broke the tense silence. Naomi flinched slightly as the needle pierced her skin, but she bit her lip and stifled any further reaction, determined to remain brave. Her eyes fixated on the clear plastic bag, watching the slow, rhythmic drip of the saline solution as it began to fill the tubing, the steady trickle becoming a small source of reassurance in the otherwise sterile and intimidating environment. Graham squeezed her hand gently, offering silent comfort, his presence a grounding force amidst the clinical decor of the room.

"Have you ever wondered how many moments pass without us noticing?" she asked quietly.

Cassidy looked up. "What do you mean?"

Naomi shrugged faintly. "Like… all the tiny ones. Every blink, every beat. Lately, I've been trying to feel them all. Even the hard ones."

Cassidy nodded. "That's a beautiful way to live. Even now."

As the last note faded away, she carefully packed her sheet music and instrument into the worn leather case. The room was filled with the faint echoes of applause, a testament to the night's performance. Turning towards Naomi, she offered a warm smile and gently placed her hand on Naomi's knee, a reassuring gesture amidst the post-show excitement. The warmth of her touch lingered a silent acknowledgment of their shared experience at that moment.

"I'll see you in a few days, okay?"

Naomi smiled. "Thank you, Cassidy."

As the last note faded away, she carefully packed her sheet music and instrument into the worn leather case. The room was filled with the faint echoes of applause, a testament to the night's performance. Turning towards Naomi, she offered a warm smile and gently placed her hand on Naomi's knee, a reassuring gesture amidst the post-show excitement. The warmth of her touch lingered a silent acknowledgment of their shared experience at that moment.

"I'm glad she comes. Makes me feel human."

"You are human," Graham whispered. "The most radiant one I know."

That sunny afternoon, Ruth and Thomas arrived at the door, beaming with excitement. Ruth held a colorful DVD case in her hands, its glossy surface reflecting the sunlight, while Thomas balanced a tray laden with an assortment of small, carefully arranged snacks. The tray featured an array of homemade treats—golden-brown miniature quiches, vibrant vegetable skewers, and delicate raspberry tarts, all artfully garnished with fresh herbs. As they stepped inside, the warm aroma of freshly baked goods filled the air, promising a delightful gathering ahead.

"We figured you could use a little comfort comedy," Ruth said, holding up Julie & Julia with a grin.

Thomas chuckled. "You always loved Julia Child's voice. Used to mimic it until we begged you to stop."

Naomi laughed. "Bon appétit!" she squeaked in a perfect imitation, and everyone groaned playfully.

Ruth carefully placed the wooden tray on the polished coffee table, arranging the snacks with a keen eye for presentation. On one side, she stacked crisp, golden crackers topped with thinly sliced turkey and sharp cheddar cheese, their savory aroma inviting and appetizing. On the other side, vibrant fruit skewers showcased an array of colors—juicy, red strawberries, sweet, succulent melon chunks, and plump, juicy grapes—all beautifully interspersed, creating a visually appealing centerpiece that beckoned to be savored.

Naomi managed three bites, chewing slowly. "That's good," she said with a small smile.

"You sure you don't want the whole tray?" Thomas

teased.

"Don't tempt me," she whispered. "I could eat the grapes and die happy."

The movie played on the screen, filling the dimly lit room with hearty laughter and a warm sense of comfort. Naomi couldn't help but giggle during Julia's perfectly chaotic kitchen disasters, her eyes sparkling with amusement as flour dusted the air in playful clouds. She leaned lightly against Ruth's side, feeling the softness of the blanket draped over them, their shared warmth amplifying the cozy atmosphere. The scent of popcorn wafted through the room, intertwining with their laughter, creating a magical moment that felt both intimate and timeless.

"This feels nice," Naomi murmured at one point. "Just this. All of us. No fixing. Just being."

As the golden hues of dusk settled over the horizon, casting elongated shadows across the landscape, Beck and Willow strolled down the gravel path toward the cozy cottage. The soft chirping of crickets began to fill the air as they approached the door. Naomi's eyes sparkled with excitement and warmth when she caught sight of them, her heart swelling with joy at the arrival of her dear friends. The gentle breeze carried the faint scent of blooming jasmine, adding to the ambiance of the evening.

"You came," she said.

Willow leaned over to kiss her cheek. "Of course we did."

Beck smiled and placed a small paper bag beside the couch. "A little something for later. Chocolate-covered almonds."

Naomi laughed. "You know my love language."

Willow sat on the edge of the coffee table, studying Naomi's face gently. "You look peaceful today."

"I feel it," Naomi said. "Tired, but not sad."

Within minutes, though, her heavy eyelids began to flutter as fatigue washed over her. The warm glow of the dim lamp cast a soft light over the room, creating a cozy atmosphere. Graham noticed her struggle to stay awake and quickly moved to his side, gently guiding her to recline against the plush sofa cushions. As he settled her more comfortably, he lovingly tucked the soft, knitted blanket around her shoulders, ensuring she felt cozy and secure as she drifted off to sleep. The faint sound of her breathing soon filled the room, a gentle reminder of her peaceful surrender to rest.

"She's sleeping more often now," he told them.

Beck nodded. "I can't imagine."

Willow placed her hand on Naomi's foot under the blanket. "She's safe. That's what matters."

Later that evening, as the house settled into a serene stillness with only the soft whispers of the night breaking the silence, Graham stepped into the living room. The pale glow of the rising moon illuminated the space through the large bay windows, casting delicate shadows across the floor. In his arms, he cradled a small, gray bundle, swaddled in a cozy blanket, its tiny form radiating warmth and fragility. The gentle rise and fall of its chest hinted at the peacefulness of slumber, while Graham couldn't help but smile, feeling a mix of joy and protectiveness wash over him in the quiet embrace of the moonlit room.

"Naomi," he whispered. "I have something for you."

She stirred, her sleep-fogged mind slowly clearing as she turned her gaze toward him. Her eyes widened in surprise, taking in the sight of the soft, tufted ears that perked up at the slightest sound, the tiny pink nose that twitched curiously, and the small gray tabby cat cradled gently in his hands. Its fur was plush and silky, glinting in the soft light, while a gentle purring rumbled in its throat, creating a soothing melody that seemed to fill the room.

"Oh," she whispered. "Oh, my goodness."

He delicately placed the tiny, gray kitten on her chest, its soft, velvety fur brushing against her skin. As if sensing her warmth, the kitten nestled snugly beneath her chin, its small body vibrating with a contented purr that sounded like a gentle motorboat humming in the distance. The rhythmic sound filled the quiet room, creating an atmosphere of comfort and tranquility.

Naomi blinked back tears. "He's perfect."

"He's ours," Graham said. "If you want him."

She nodded, breath catching. "What should we name him?"

He sat beside her, rubbing the kitten's back. "You choose."

Naomi studied the tiny creature, then whispered, "Milo."

Graham smiled. "Milo it is."

Milo meowed softly, his soft fur glistening in the gentle afternoon light as he curled into the warmth of Naomi's lap. She stroked his head tenderly, her fingers gently gliding over his ears while a faint tremor of emotion laced her voice. The quiet room was filled with a sense of peace, punctuated only by the rhythmic sound of Milo's purring, creating a cocoon of comfort around them both.

"Thank you, Graham. For knowing what I need

before I do."

He kissed her hand. "I've had practice."

As the soft, rhythmic purring of the kitten reverberated in the tranquil room and the world outside faded into a gentle hush, Naomi leaned back into Graham's warm embrace. She cradled the tiny creature in one hand, feeling its delicate heartbeat against her palm, a symbol of new beginnings and hope. On the other hand, she let go of the swirling fears that had haunted her, allowing the comforting presence of Graham and the innocence of the kitten to wash over her like a soothing balm.

Chapter Twenty: What Love Does

When the last day of July arrived, a heavy weight settled within Naomi, a stark reminder that her body was no longer her own. She could feel it in the leaden heaviness of her limbs, each movement sapping her dwindling strength. Her breath came in shallow, labored gasps as if her lungs were struggling to keep pace with the relentless passage of time. Once a vibrant source of joy and comfort, food had transformed into a bland obligation; each meal became a daunting task rather than a delight. Most days, she managed only a few hesitant bites, sometimes less. She would force down a quarter of a rich, nutritional Ensure and sip at the colorful smoothies that Graham lovingly crafted each morning—blends of berries, greens, and protein designed to nourish her but which now felt like an insurmountable chore. The vibrant flavors that once danced on her palate now slipped away into a dull echo of necessity, underscoring the growing dissonance between her body and spirit.

Today, a velvety blend of ripe peaches and creamy almond milk swirled with crushed ice sat before her, infused with a whisper of gentle hope. The vibrant hues of the drink shimmered in the afternoon sunlight as Graham handed her the delicate glass, its cool surface glistening with condensation. He settled beside her on the worn wooden bench, savoring his drink—a subtle reminder of their shared moment.

Graham watched intently as she brought the glass to her lips, taking a slow sip that lingered, a subtle smile spreading across her face. But as she set the glass down, her expression shifted; a flicker of guilt danced in her eyes, mingling with the moment's sweetness. She smiled at him, a mix of warmth and unspoken regret as if trying to reconcile the joy of their shared drink with the weight of what lay unsaid between them.

"I'm sorry," she whispered.

He shook his head. "You tried. That's enough."

Naomi set the glass down and leaned her head on his shoulder. "It's not just the food. It's everything. I can feel it, Graham… this is different."

He wrapped his arm around her and pulled her close. "I know."

Later that morning, Naomi sat before the ornate vanity mirror, its vintage frame reflecting the soft morning light streaming through the window. A delicate brush, with bristles worn yet gentle, rested in her hand. As she glided the brush through her once-lustrous hair —now reduced to fine silk strands that caught the light —her fingers trembled ever so slightly, a reminder of the changes she had faced. With each stroke, she felt the weight of the strands that slipped free, the brush quickly filling with a cascade of silvery hair. Naomi stared at the clump for a long moment, a mix of disbelief and resignation washing over her, before she placed the brush down with a sigh, the soft thud breaking the room's stillness.

She didn't move to hide the hair. She just stared at herself.

When Graham stepped into the softly lit room, his gaze immediately settled on the worn wooden brush resting on the small vanity, its bristles slightly frayed from years of use. After a fleeting moment, his eyes shifted to her face, which had turned slightly away, framed by cascading locks of hair that glimmered in the sunlight streaming through the window. Without uttering a word, he moved silently behind her, the air charged with unspoken feelings between them. He reached for the brush, its cool handle fitting comfortably in his palm, then ran it gently through her hair, savoring the tactile sensation as the strands glided effortlessly against the bristles. Each stroke was careful and deliberate, revealing tender moments of closeness that silently spoke volumes.

Naomi closed her eyes. "You always do it so carefully."

"I'm afraid I'll hurt you," he said quietly.

"You won't."

She opened her eyes and glanced into the mirror, catching a fleeting glimpse of him in the corner of her vision. He was making a clumsy attempt to conceal the brush, its bristles now thickly coated with vibrant paint once again. The bright hues spilled over the edges, a stark contrast against the polished wood of the vanity. But it was too late—she had already witnessed the truth of his actions reflected in her own wide eyes.

"I see it," she said softly.

He met her eyes. "Then see this, too."

He gently leaned down, his warm lips brushing against the soft strands of her hair as he placed a tender kiss on the crown of her head, the familiar, comforting scent of her shampoo enveloping him in a moment of quiet intimacy.

It happened quickly, instantly sending a chill down Graham's spine. Naomi had insisted, with her usual determination, that she could navigate the short distance to the bathroom independently. Her confidence reassured him, so he turned to the kitchen, intending to rinse out her unfinished smoothie glass, the bright pink hue still swirling at the bottom. Just as he set the glass beneath the cool stream of water, he heard it—the fall. It wasn't loud, more of a soft thud that disrupted the quiet of their small apartment, followed by an unsettling stillness that seemed to hang in the air. A rush of concern flooded through him as he dropped the glass into the sink, the sound of it clinking against the ceramic barely registering as he raced down the hallway, dread tightening in his chest.

"Naomi!" he shouted, running into the hallway.

She lay crumpled near the doorframe, her once-vibrant dress now tattered and dusty, eyes fluttering as if struggling to focus on the dim light filtering through the cracked doorway. The faint scent of damp wood surrounded her, mingling with the lingering echoes of muted voices from the rooms beyond. Her breath came in shallow gasps. Each exhale mingled with the stillness of the air, creating a stark contrast to the chaos that had just unfolded.

"I... I'm okay," she whispered.

"No, you're not," Graham said, scooping her into his arms.

She felt weightless as if suspended in a boundless sea of air. The gentle breeze brushed against her skin, lifting her hair and wrapping her in a soft embrace. With each breath, she sensed the freedom of floating from the burdens of the world below. Her heart raced with exhilaration, and for a moment, time seemed to pause, allowing her to savor the liberation that enveloped her like a warm glow.

He swiftly snatched his worn leather wallet, the familiar jingle of his keys, and the sleek, cold phone surface with one hand while his other arm securely wrapped around her waist. The moment's urgency left no room for hesitation; they had to move quickly. His heart raced violently, pounding in his throat with a mix of adrenaline and fear. Each breath felt electric, heightened by the weight of their situation.

The drive to Cape Regional Medical Center felt disorienting, with a chaotic swirl of flashing red lights and the hurried chatter of emergency responders. The antiseptic scent filled the air as they sped past, each siren wailing like a desperate plea for help. He leaned closer to her, gripping her hand tightly, his heart racing with anxiety. "Stay with me," he murmured, his voice wavering urgently. "Please stay with me." He searched her eyes for signs of awareness, his mind racing with memories of happier times, unwilling to let go of hope even as the world outside rushed by in a blur.

Inside the bustling emergency department, the nurse stationed at the front desk glanced down at Naomi's chart, her expression shifting to one of concern. With a soft tone, she looked up and asked gently, "Hospice?" The word hung in the air, a reminder of the gravity of the situation, as the sounds of pagers and distant conversations faded momentarily around them.

Graham nodded. "I didn't know what to do. She fell. I panicked."

"You did the right thing," the nurse said. Her name tag read Mara Kellis, who is calm and compassionate in her mid-30s. We'll take care of her."

Naomi was gently wheeled into a softly lit hospital

room, the faint scent of antiseptic hanging in the air. A nurse carefully attached a pulse oximeter to her finger, the small device beeping rhythmically as it monitored her vital signs. An oxygen cannula was snugly fitted under her nose, delivering a steady flow of oxygen to ease her breathing. As she drifted in and out of consciousness, her eyelids fluttered, and she murmured Graham's name, a whisper of longing that echoed through the sterile surroundings whenever she stirred.

Minutes later, a physician entered the dimly lit room. In his early 40s, Dr. Caleb Irwin wore navy scrubs neatly tucked under a crisp white coat, the fabric slightly wrinkled from a long day. His deep-set, hazel eyes reflected a quiet empathy that only those who have witnessed profound sorrow can genuinely possess. The slight weariness etched on his face spoke volumes about the countless emotional battles he fought daily in his line of work. His voice was soft and gentle when he spoke, each word carefully chosen as if to offer solace amidst the chaos.

"Mr. Jameson?" he asked, shaking Graham's hand. "I'm Dr. Irwin. I've reviewed Naomi's chart. She's under hospice care—yes?"

Graham nodded, running a hand through his hair. "I didn't mean to break protocol. I just… I couldn't see her like that."

Dr. Irwin placed a reassuring hand on his shoulder. "You did what love does. You protected her."

He turned to the nurse. "Let's start an IV: fluids—Lactated Ringers, one liter. Add Zofran for nausea and a low-dose morphine infusion. Comfort care levels."

He looked back at Graham. "Her vitals are weak but stable. We'll keep her comfortable, and then arrange for her to return home. We can do nothing to stop what's happening... but we can make sure it isn't painful."

Graham swallowed hard. "Thank you."

Dr. Irwin paused. "We'll notify her hospice nurse. She'll be discharged as soon as she's ready."

It was late afternoon when they finally left the bustling emergency room, the fluorescent lights behind them flickering like distant stars. Graham carefully lifted Naomi, cradling her fragile form in his arms, and guided her toward the car parked under the fading light of the setting sun. As he settled her into the passenger seat, he noticed her head rested heavily against the window, her eyelids fluttering gently as though she were caught between sleep and waking. The soft hum of the engine faded into the background as she took slow, shallow breaths, the rhythmic rise and fall of her chest a stark reminder of her exhaustion and the ordeal they had just endured.

"Graham?" she murmured.

"I'm here."

"Thank you... for not letting go."

He kissed her lips. "Never."

As he navigated the winding road home, one hand firmly grasping the steering wheel while the other lovingly entwined with hers, Naomi was drifting in and out of sleep. The soft hum of the engine and the rhythmic sway of the car created a soothing lullaby, causing her eyelids to grow heavy. The warm glow of the dashboard lights flickered gently, illuminating their faces in fleeting bursts, while the scent of the fresh pine trees outside wafted in through the slightly open window, mingling with the faint aroma of their shared dinner. Each gentle bump in the road and the comforting presence of his hand made her feel safe and cherished, yet the day's fatigue tugged at her consciousness, pulling her into a dreamlike state.

He gripped his phone with trembling fingers at the glaring red light, the weight of urgency pressing down on him. He quickly typed out four texts, each message a lifeline amid chaos.

Ruth: *"We were in the ER. She fell hard from the stairs. She's home now, but the doctors say it's worse than we thought."*

Beck: *"Please come as soon as you can. I need you here; I can't do this alone."*

Jennifer: *"Mom... she's slipping away from us. I don't know how much longer we have."*

Willow: *"Can you come to Ruth and Thomas' tonight? We need your support; I don't know how to handle this without you."*

Each text sent was a poignant blend of desperation and hope, weaving together the profound sense of isolation that enveloped them and the comforting warmth of connection with loved ones. Each message was urgent, revealing intimate thoughts and silent fears, while also expressing a longing for reassurance and understanding from distant hearts. The flicker of a screen became a lifeline, transforming solitary moments into shared experiences, as words traveled across the miles, bridging the emotional chasm that threatened to engulf them.

That evening, the warm glow of soft lamplight spilled from Ruth and Thomas' home, casting gentle shadows on the familiar walls as friends and family began to gather. The aroma of freshly baked bread wafted through the air, mingling with the comforting scent of brewed tea. Jennifer arrived first, her usually vibrant face now a shade paler than usual, yet she held herself with a composed grace. As she stepped inside, her eyes reflected grief and determination. She immediately moved towards Graham, enveloping him in a tight embrace that spoke volumes of their shared sorrow and support. The sound of her soft sobs filled the entryway, a reminder of the love they all held for Naomi.

"She's tired," Graham said. "So tired. I carry her more than she walks."

Ruth placed a hand on her chest. "I feel like my lungs are heavy just hearing it."

Beck came in next, followed by Willow. They didn't speak immediately—they just joined the group in the living room, where tea had been brewed, but no one drank it.

"She still smiles," Graham said after a long silence. "She's still Naomi. Just... slower. Quieter."

Willow's eyes filled with tears. "I don't know how to say goodbye to someone who's still here."

"You don't," Jennifer whispered. "You just love her louder."

Thomas sat quietly in the dimly lit corner of the room, his hands clenched tightly into fists, knuckles pale against the worn fabric of his jeans. The air was thick with tension, and the hushed murmurs of the others seemed to fade into the background. He hadn't spoken yet, but when he finally did, his voice emerged low and shaky, cutting through the silence like a knife. The impact of his words shattered the stillness, leaving everyone in stunned silence, their eyes wide and focused solely on him.

"She's my little girl."

Ruth leaned into him and held his hand. "I know, love. I know."

Beck cleared his throat. "If there's anything we can do…"

"You're already doing it," Graham replied. "You showed up."

The room was still, enveloped in a heavy silence that seemed to hang like a thick fog. Dust particles danced lazily in the shafts of pale light filtering through the half-drawn curtains, their delicate movements contrasting with the quietude. Shadows pooled in the corners, hinting at forgotten memories, while the scent of aged wood and faint floral notes lingered, creating a nostalgic and slightly eerie atmosphere.

Then Graham stood, his voice low but steady. "I'm keeping her home. I don't care how hard it gets. I won't send her away. Not when every day might be our last."

No one argued. No one needed to. They sat in the room's dim light, a soft glow from the flickering candles casting gentle shadows on their faces. Each person was enveloped in their thoughts, yet their silence spoke volumes. They were bound together in their shared grief, arms resting across each other's shoulders, the warmth of their presence a fragile comfort amidst the heartache.

Outside, the wind whispered through the trees, a haunting melody that seemed to echo their sorrow. Something sacred settled around them in that quiet moment—a palpable sense of connection and understanding. It was the knowing—that profound awareness of their love for what was lost and for one another. The waiting felt heavy, yet sacred, as they embraced the ache that accompanied their shared memories. It was the aching beauty of love that endures beyond loss, intertwining their souls in a tapestry of remembrance, hope, and unyielding support.

Chapter Twenty-One: The Deepest Kind of Love

Later, on July 31, 2024, the air inside the house had taken on a sacred stillness—an almost reverential hush, as if even the walls were aware of the gravity of the moment unfolding within their confines. Naomi lay beneath a soft, pale linen blanket that barely rose and fell with her light and shallow breath, each exhalation a gentle reminder of her fragility. The delicate hum of her IV pump provided the only sound, a rhythmic companion to the occasional rustle of Milo, her loyal cat, shifting restlessly against her leg, his warmth seeking comfort in the stillness. Sunlight filtered through the sheer curtains, spilling in like ribbons of gold, casting gentle patterns across the room; yet, rather than invigorating the space, it merely offered a fragile warmth, a bittersweet reminder of the vibrant life that once filled the room.

At her bedside sat Elena Marks, her hospice nurse, a steady hand in the uncertain landscape of illness and fragility. Elena, in her mid-fifties, embodied a quiet strength. Her auburn hair, elegantly swept into a neat bun, showcased gentle waves that glimmered under the soft bedside lamp. Her hazel eyes, warm and inviting, seemed to hold a wealth of understanding and compassion, reflecting a lifetime of stories and experiences.

She approached each day with a calm demeanor, never imposing comfort but rather offering it like a carefully brewed cup of tea—gentle, soothing, and ready to be savored. The faint scent of lavender lingered around her, a subtle reminder of her dedication to creating a peaceful environment. In those delicate moments, she patiently sat, her presence a comforting presence, allowing the quiet to envelop the room until it was time for words to join the stillness. Elena checked Naomi's vitals, her pen stilling on the chart as she looked at her patient.

"You're doing okay," she said quietly. "Numbers are low but steady."

Naomi stared at the ceiling, her voice no more than a whisper. "You know Graham didn't just run an errand."

Elena set her clipboard aside, giving her full attention. "No. I know."

Naomi blinked slowly. "He needed space. Somewhere to go… because watching me fade is breaking him. He doesn't say it, but I see it in his eyes every time he pulls my blanket up."

Elena felt a deep, aching sorrow for both of them, her heart heavy with compassion as she watched them struggle through their pain. The weight of their shared misery pressed against her chest, making it hard to breathe, and she wished there was something—anything —she could do to ease their burdens.

Naomi turned her head slightly. "I don't want to do this to him anymore. I want to go to inpatient hospice."

Elena paused, her expression softening. "That's a big decision, Naomi."

"I know," Naomi said. "But it's time. He deserves

peace, too."

Just then, Milo, still a small bundle of fur but growing at a surprising rate, leaped onto the bed with an energetic spring. He curled up beside her hip, his soft purring resonating like a steady, soothing heartbeat. Naomi reached down to lift him into her arms, her fingers brushing against his warm, velvety coat, but her hand trembled with a mix of fatigue and emotion, ultimately dropping back to the quilted surface of the bed. The comforting weight of Milo beside her contrasted with the heaviness in her heart, reminding her of the simple joys that remained in her life.

A tear slipped from the corner of her eye. "He's too heavy for me now."

She pet Milo softly, fingers shaking. "I'm ready to die, Elena. Not because I'm giving up—but because I've been so fully, wholly loved."

Elena moved closer, wrapping her hand around Naomi's. "Then let's make this sacred. Not just quiet—but meaningful."

Naomi's voice cracked. "Please take care of Graham. When I'm gone... please make sure someone holds him like he's held me."

"I promise," Elena whispered. "I promise."

Across town, Graham stepped into the warm, welcoming environment of Ruth and Thomas' cozy home. The aroma of freshly brewed coffee wafted through the air, mingling with the faint scent of cinnamon from the apple pie cooling on the kitchen counter. This home, adorned with family photographs and soft, inviting furnishings, was where the heart of their family often gathered. It provided a refuge from the chaotic outside world, where laughter and stories flowed freely and where the weight of life's burdens felt lighter when shared among loved ones.

He was pale, his skin almost ghostly, dark shadows pooling under his eyes, now rimmed red like a sunset drowning in sorrow. Ruth instinctively reached for him, wrapping her arms around him in a tight embrace, feeling the tremor of his body against hers. The warmth of her presence was a stark contrast to the heavy chill in the air. Jennifer, Beck, and Willow stood nearby, forming quiet circles of shared grief, their expressions a tapestry of disbelief and pain. The unspoken truth lingered in the room, heavy like a folded flag draped over a casket, a somber reminder of the loss that had brought them together in this moment of mourning.

"She's tired," Graham said. "And I think... we're almost there."

A heavy silence enveloped the room, an unspoken tension hanging in the air like a thick fog. No one exchanged glances or murmured reassuring words; each person remained rooted in their thoughts, grappling with their emotions. The moment's gravity was palpable as if the collective weight of their shared experience rendered them speechless. No one needed to break the stillness; the silence spoke volumes, conveying understanding, uncertainty, and a profound sense of connection that words would have only diluted.

"She still smiles when she sees Milo. But she's barely eating. She's slipping away in pieces. And I keep wondering if there's more I can do."

"You've done everything," Jennifer whispered. "And more."

Ruth wiped her eyes. "Then maybe... we do something for her now. Something she can hold onto."

163

They gathered around the cozy kitchen table, its worn surface gleaming under the soft glow of the hanging light. The scent of freshly brewed coffee filled the air as they spread out colorful maps and blueprints, their faces illuminated with anticipation and determination. Laughter and murmurs of excitement intertwined with a ticking clock, heightening the urgency as they meticulously plotted their next steps. Each person brought unique ideas to the table, their pens scratching against paper as they scribbled notes and sketched out plans, united in their goal yet each adding their vision to the mix.

A memory scrapbook was the winning idea, and everyone agreed it was the best decision for Naomi and Graham. Ruth and Thomas: Naomi's childhood—finger-paintings, beach days, stories about her stubborn little will. Willow: Their teenage years—sailing for the first time, sleepovers, poetry scribbled in notebooks. Graham: Their love—how they met, broke apart, and found each other again. Beck: Their marriage—photographs, gentle mornings, Naomi's smile tucked into every corner of the house. Jennifer: The assembler—the one to pull it all together in blue and white, Naomi's favorite colors.

Beck looked at Graham. "We'll give her the best of us. So she knows she was never alone."

The sun dipped below a blanket of soft, cottony clouds, casting a warm, golden hue across the room as Elena gently pushed the door open to return to Naomi's space. The room was infused with a fresh, soothing scent from the warm sponge bath she had just given, and Naomi now wore a fresh, soft cotton gown that clung lightly to her skin. Milo, their loyal kitten, was curled up in his usual corner, his tail thumping softly against the floor in contentment. Looking out the window, Naomi seemed lost in thought, her eyes tracking the slow dance of shadows as the sky transitioned into twilight.

"Does dying hurt?" she asked suddenly.

Elena sat down beside her, resting a hand on her arm. "It's like a tide going out. Not all at once. But little by little, the noise quiets. And then you're floating."

Naomi let the silence linger. "I just don't want it to be scary."

"It won't be," Elena said gently. "Because you'll never be alone."

A gentle, almost hesitant knock echoed from the front door, its sound mingling with the soft rustle of leaves outside. The late afternoon sunlight cast a warm glow, illuminating the doormat where shadows danced, hinting at the presence of an unexpected visitor. Elena rose to answer it and opened the door to Pastor Eli Whitcomb, dressed in soft gray slacks, his shirt pressed, and his Bible held gently.

"Pastor," Elena greeted. "She's been waiting for you."

He nodded slowly, the moment's weight settling over him, and stepped inside with a reverent quiet that felt palpable in the air. The bedroom was dimly lit, the soft glow of a bedside lamp casting gentle shadows on the walls. As he entered, he caught sight of Naomi, her expression transforming instantly; her eyes lit up like stars in an ink-black sky, brimming with a mixture of surprise and delight that filled the room with warmth.

"Pastor," she whispered.

He took her hand and smiled. "May I read to you?"

"Yes… please."

He opened his worn Bible, the leather cover creased from years of use, and inhaled deeply, letting the familiar scent of aged paper fill his lungs. He began to read with a deep and steady voice, his words resonating in the quiet room, each verse echoing with the weight of wisdom and reflection. The sunlight streamed through the stained glass windows, casting colorful patterns on the wooden pews as he intently shared the powerful messages within the sacred pages.

Naomi let out a trembling breath, her chest rising and falling in a rhythm of anxiety, and nodded slowly, her eyes glistening with unshed tears. Pastor Whitcomb leaned in closer, his gaze piercing yet compassionate as he looked directly into her eyes, searching for the turmoil beneath her calm exterior. The dim light of the room cast gentle shadows, emphasizing the worry etched on her face.

"The Lord is nigh unto them that are of a broken heart;
and saveth such as be of a contrite spirit." (Psalm 34:18)

Then he bowed his head. "Let us pray." Then he spoke,
"Heavenly Father,
We thank You for the life of Naomi—the tenderness in her touch, the laughter in her voice, and the love she has poured into the hearts of everyone she's met.
We lift her pain to You and ask that You replace it with peace.
We ask for comfort in the moments ahead—for strength where there is sorrow, for breath where there is fear, for light where there is darkness.
Hold her hand, Lord, and when she can no longer walk, carry her gently home.
And for Graham—her anchor and heart—wrap him in Your presence.

May he know that love never ends.
In Jesus' name, we pray,
Amen."

Naomi sat on the edge of the worn armchair, her shoulders shaking as tears streamed silently down her face. The dim light of the room cast elongated shadows on the walls, accentuating the heavy air of grief that hung around her. As her sobs faded into whispers, she felt the weight of the silence enveloping her, punctuated only by the faint ticking of an old clock in the corner. The stillness felt suffocating, a reminder of the absence that now filled the space where laughter once resonated.

"You are not alone," Pastor Whitcomb said as he kissed her hand. "Not now. Not ever."

That evening, the front door creaked open once more, letting a chill breeze sweep into the warm glow of the foyer. Graham stepped inside, his boots softly thudding against the polished wooden floor as he brushed off remnants of the chilly autumn air. His gaze immediately locked onto Naomi, who stood by the staircase, a soft light framing her silhouette. She offered him a faint smile, a mix of relief and uncertainty flickering across her face as she tucked a stray lock of hair behind her ear.

"Did you find what you were looking for?" she asked.

He settled onto the plush couch beside her, feeling the warmth radiate from her presence. Gently, he placed a small, elegantly wrapped box, tied with a delicate satin ribbon, on her lap. The box glimmered softly in the warm light, hinting at the thoughtfulness of its contents, as a sense of anticipation hung between them. A luxurious blue satin robe was nestled inside the delicate packaging, its soft fabric glimmering subtly in the light. Her initials, elegantly monogrammed in a flowing script near the collar, added a personal touch that brought a smile to her face. Just above the heart, a tiny embroidered sea-glass heart shimmered like a piece of ocean treasure, evoking memories of tranquil beach walks and whispered secrets by the shore.

Naomi's hands trembled as she gently caressed the fabric, feeling the smoothness beneath her fingertips. A wave of nostalgia washed over her.

"It's beautiful," she whispered.

"You are," Graham said. "I just wanted you wrapped in something that feels like home."

She reached for his face, brushing his cheek. "You've given me so much, Graham. I'm not afraid."

He kissed her forehead and whispered, "I know."

Outside, the stars blinked into existence, twinkling like distant diamonds against the velvety night sky. Inside that quiet house, Naomi lay nestled in a cocoon of soft blankets, surrounded by the warmth of love—her family's laughter still echoing faintly in the background. The gentle hum of the world outside faded into a serene whisper, wrapping her in a blanket of peace. Flickering candlelight cast playful shadows on the walls, creating a cozy ambiance that felt almost magical. She wasn't alone. Not now, with the whispers of cherished memories lingering in the air. Not ever, with the unwavering support of those who adored her, eternally close to her heart.

Chapter Twenty-Two: The Last Page

The house was enveloped in tranquil silence, broken only by the gentle ticking of the kitchen clock, its rhythmic sound echoing softly throughout the space, and the quiet, steady hum of the air conditioner, which fought valiantly against the warm morning air. Sunlight filtered through the sheer, pale curtains, casting a soft golden glow that warmed the room without overwhelming it—almost as if the world outside had sensed the need for peace and chose to whisper instead of shout. Jennifer sat at the dining table, her fingers gliding slowly and deliberately across the pages of an open scrapbook, which rested like a treasure chest overflowing with memories. Each page was densely packed—so full that it resisted closure, the colorful edges threatening to spill over. She paused on the final spread, her fingertips tracing the delicate lines of Ruth's careful handwriting that chronicled Naomi's childhood—words that captured fleeting moments, like the times they had sat in the garden, surrounded by flowers, laughter, and sunshine. Scattered among the text were little crayon drawings from kindergarten, vibrant depictions of stick figures and suns, a testament to innocent days.

As she flipped to another sheet, Willow's spirited stories from their teenage years unfolded across the paper—tales of adventurous sailing trips where high winds and laughter echoed, sunburns that left memories etched in pink skin, and the thrill of sharing first secrets under starry skies. Beck's contributions came next: a collection of photographs that captured the essence of joyous occasions—the warmth of their wedding day, the exhilaration of a boat ride cutting through shimmering waters, and quiet moments spent on the porch at dusk, where golden light met the horizon in a breathtaking embrace. Each page not only showcased memories but also wove together the threads of their lives, telling a story of connection, love, and the passage of time.

And there was Graham's entry—a handwritten letter, its edges neatly creased, suggesting careful folding. The parchment bore the subtle, aged scent of ink and paper, hinting at the time taken to compose each word. It lay there untouched by anyone else's hands, a personal artifact that hinted at intimate thoughts and emotions, waiting patiently to reveal its secrets. Jennifer's throat tightened as she reached for the last sticker—a tiny sea-glass heart. She pressed it into the corner of the page in a slow, deliberate motion; she closed the book, the sound of its cover softly thudding against the spine, breaking the silence of the dimly lit room.

She lingered for a moment, her fingers tracing the embossed title on the front as if savoring the journey she had just completed. The final page, filled with the last words of the story, remained vivid in her mind, echoing with emotion. It felt as though an entire world had just slipped away, leaving her with a bittersweet sense of closure. The book was finished, but its impact would linger long after the final closing.

At Jameson & Co. Woodworks, Miles Harper leaned

over a weathered oak workbench, his brow furrowed in concentration, the quiet hum of machinery filling the air. His hands, rough and calloused, were dusted with fine sawdust that caught the warm beams of sunlight streaming through the overhead windows. The rich, earthy aroma of freshly cut cedar mingled with the scent of varnish, creating an atmosphere ripe with the promise of new beginnings and creative potential. This workshop, filled with the gentle sounds of woodworking tools and the soft rustle of wood shavings, was his sanctuary now —at least until Graham returned. If he ever returned. Doubts swirled in Miles's mind like the curls of wood he crafted, each thought more tangled than the last, as he considered the uncertainty of their future.

Chloe arrived just before noon, her strawberry-blonde hair elegantly styled in a loose braid that cascaded over her shoulder, catching the sunlight in soft, golden hues. Clutched in her hand was a slightly crumpled brown paper bag from The Seaside Café, its edges stained with faint coffee rings, hinting at the delicious pastries and fresh sandwiches nestled inside. The warm, salty breeze from the nearby ocean tousled her hair as she walked, a smile spreading across her face in anticipation of the lunch ahead.

"You're a menace," Miles teased as she stepped inside.

"You're a martyr for trying to live off coffee and chips," she replied, handing him a sandwich and sitting on the edge of the desk.

They sat at a rustic wooden table, the faint aroma of their homemade meal wafting between them. The muted glow of the candle flickered softly, casting warm shadows on their faces as they enjoyed their meal in peaceful companionship. Their comfortable silence felt like a shared language, one that did not require constant chatter to fill the air. Each bite was savored, and the gentle clinking of utensils was the only sound that broke the tranquility, creating an atmosphere rich with unspoken understanding and connection.

Chloe placed her hand on his. "You're doing great, you know."

He nodded, staring at a half-finished sketch of a memory box on his desk. "I just want to make something that matters."

"You already are."

Beck sat at his worn kitchen table, the warm light of the late afternoon sun streaming through the window, casting a gentle glow on the scattered photographs before him. Across from him, Willow's fingers brushed against his as they flipped through the treasured snapshots, each image evoking a swell of memories. They carefully arranged the photos into a second memory book—an unexpected gift for Graham in the wake of Naomi's passing. The table was cluttered with remnants of their shared history: an empty mug of chamomile tea, a few crumpled napkins, and a fading notebook filled with handwritten notes. With each photo they selected, they exchanged quiet glances and soft smiles, a bittersweet connection forged in their shared loss.

"Look at her in this one," Willow whispered, pointing to a shot of Naomi laughing with wind in her hair. "She looks… so alive."

"She was always more alive than the rest of us," Beck said, his voice tight.

They grew quiet, enveloped in a stillness that held both an undeniable comfort and an unbearable weight.

The air between them thickened, punctuated only by the distant hum of life outside. Willow reached for a roll of double-sided tape, her fingers trembling as they hovered above the sleek surface. Just as the tape slipped slightly from her grasp, Beck gently took it from her hand, his touch warm and reassuring. Their eyes met, a moment frozen in time, and they didn't look away for the first time in what felt like ages.

Beck leaned in, his heart racing, as he brushed a loose strand of Willow's chestnut hair behind her ear. The simple act felt charged, like an electric current passing between them. Then, with a mixture of uncertainty and yearning, he kissed her—soft, hesitant, and honest. The world around them faded, leaving only the warmth of shared breath and the soft whisper of their longing. Willow let herself be kissed. Because sometimes, even in the ache, there's room for something new.

Ruth had spread out an array of old photos across the living room floor, transforming the space into a nostalgic gallery of memories. Boxes filled with Polaroids from the '90s lay scattered among neatly stacked school pictures, vivid birthday party snapshots featuring lopsided cakes, and wide, gap-toothed smiles that captured the innocence of childhood. Naomi's beloved baby blanket, with its soft, worn fabric and faded pastel colors, was draped over the back of the sofa, a gentle reminder of her early years. Thomas sat cross-legged, carefully inspecting a photograph resting in his lap—an image of Naomi at five years old, her oversized eyes sparkling with youthful wonder, her hair styled in playful pigtails that framed her face. The atmosphere was thick with nostalgia as each image sparked a flood of memories, weaving together the fabric of their family's history.

"She was so small," he said.

"She was mighty," Ruth replied.

Thomas's shoulders began to shake, a subtle tremor at first, as a wave of emotion surged through him, tightening his chest. The weight of his thoughts pressed heavily on him, and he could feel the warmth of tears welling up in his eyes, threatening to spill over. Each shuddering breath he took echoed his inner turmoil, a silent struggle that rippled through his body, betraying the vulnerability he fought so hard to conceal.

"I'm not ready," he whispered. "I'm not ready to lose my little girl."

Ruth crawled over beside him, her movements deliberate and gentle as she nestled up against him. She wrapped her arms around his chest, feeling the warmth of his body through the soft fabric of his shirt. The faint scent of his cologne mixed with the lingering coolness of the evening air, creating a comforting cocoon around them. As she leaned her head against his shoulder, she could hear the steady rhythm of his heart, a soothing backdrop to the quiet moment they shared.

"I know," she whispered. "I know, love."

Thomas carefully unscrewed the cap of his pill bottle, the familiar sound of the plastic rattling in his hands fading into the background. He retrieved an anti-anxiety tablet and let it rest on his tongue for a moment before washing it down with a sip of lukewarm tea, the liquid nearly tepid from sitting too long. The aroma of chamomile filled the air, but it did little to soothe his frayed nerves.

Ruth, ever patient and supportive, wrapped her arms around him, offering a steady warmth as he let out the pent-up anguish in shaky sobs. She stroked his back gently, creating a rhythm that seemed to anchor him. Gradually, as the storm of emotion subsided, his trembling eased and he found a moment of stillness, nestled against her comforting presence.

That evening, the house Graham had built for them felt impossibly quiet, as if the very walls were holding their breath. Naomi lay in bed, wrapped in her soft blue robe, the fabric soothing against her skin. The gentle glow from the bedside lamp cast warm shadows around the room, highlighting the gentle curves of the furniture and the photographs on the walls that told their story. Milo, their fluffy tabby cat, was nestled against her leg, his rhythmic purring a steady heartbeat in the silence, offering her comfort in the stillness.

Graham entered the room carrying a small wooden tray, its surface polished to a gleaming sheen. On it rested two steaming glasses of ginger tea, the aromatic warmth wafting up and filling the air with a hint of spice. Beside the glasses lay a handful of crackers, neatly arranged, though Naomi knew she likely wouldn't eat them. The familiar sound of the tray gently placed on the bedside table broke the silence, and as she looked up, she found Graham's eyes filled with a soft, caring light that made her heart swell.

Naomi smiled faintly. "Still trying?"

He sat beside her. "Still hoping."

She reached for his hand, her fingers gently brushing against his warm skin, and he enveloped her hand within both of his, his grip firm yet reassuring. The weight of their connection lingered in the air, a silent promise shared between them.

"I have something for us tonight," he whispered,

turning toward the dresser.

He carefully retrieved the wedding video from the shelf and set the laptop down on the plush comforter of the bed. As he opened the lid, Naomi felt her heart race; the screen flickered to life, revealing a soft glow that illuminated the room. The soothing sound of waves crashing against the shore filled the air, intertwining with the delicate notes of Layla's violin, which floated gently like a memory. Naomi's breath hitched as Ruth's voice broke through—a mix of tears and pride—as she began to introduce her daughter, her words imbued with deep emotion. Then came the moment they had all been waiting for: the couple's vows, filled with promises of love and hope, echoing softly through the room.

"I promise to love you even when the days are short and your hands shake.
I promise to remember that love outlives time."

Naomi stood before the mirror, taking in her own reflection as she articulated those words. The smile that stretched across her face was luminous, radiating a warmth that could light up the dim room. Her voice, steady and strong, carried a confidence that resonated with clarity, echoing off the walls like a melodious note. She could feel the energy of her words, each syllable infused with determination, as if they held the power to inspire not just herself, but anyone who might be listening. The moment felt electric, charged with the possibility of hope and empowerment.

"I meant every word," she whispered.

Graham reached up and stroked her cheek. "I know."

As the video neared its end—waves crashing rhythmically against the rugged shoreline, sunlight casting a warm, golden hue over the scene—Naomi's breathing slowed, mirroring the ebb and flow of the ocean. The salty breeze wafted through the air, carrying with it the distant cries of seagulls and the scent of seaweed. She felt a sense of calm wash over her, the chaos of everyday life fading away as she focused on the serene beauty unfolding before her.

Graham turned to kiss her temple, whispering, "I'll always be your husband."

But something had changed. The steady rise and fall of her chest had ceased, replaced by an unsettling stillness that enveloped the room. Her lips, slightly parted as if she had been about to speak, hung motionless, betraying no hint of the warmth that had once been there. Graham froze, his heart pounding in his chest as disbelief washed over him. The vibrant spark that had filled her eyes was now absent, leaving behind an eerie emptiness that sent a chill down his spine.

"Naomi?" he said softly, leaning closer.

She didn't stir.

His voice cracked. "Baby?"

No response came from her. He reached for her wrist, his fingers trembling with a mixture of urgency and fear. The coolness of her skin contrasted sharply with the warmth of his own hand, but there was no pulse—nothing to reassure him that she was still there. Desperation clawed at his gut as he struggled to steady himself, heart racing in the suffocating silence surrounding them.

"No…" he whispered, voice splintering. "No, no, no. Oh God. Oh baby, no."

He pulled her gently into his arms, holding her frail frame against his chest. "I wasn't ready. I wasn't ready…"

His sobs filled the room—desperate, raw, grieving

love pouring out.

Milo, the delicate tabby cat with glossy fur, leaped gracefully onto Graham's lap, settling in comfortably against the warmth of Naomi's plush, lavender robe. He nestled his small head into the soft fabric, purring softly as he blinked up at them with wide, emerald-green eyes. It was as if he sensed the shift in the atmosphere, a palpable change that hung in the air like the sweet scent of blooming flowers. At that moment, he seemed to understand that love had just turned a page, marking the beginning of something beautiful and new.

The scrapbook lay on the oak table, its leather cover gently worn and slightly dusted, a testament to the years gone by. With its pages packed full of vibrant photographs and delicate mementos, the cover now rested closed, heavy with the weight of cherished memories. Flipping to the last page, you'd find it wasn't blank or empty; instead, it cradled a beautiful, handwritten note adorned with doodles and flourishes. This page held the truest promise of all: Love remembered through laughter and tears. Love endured through trials and triumphs. Love, forever promised—an echo of heartfelt moments that would linger in time.

Chapter Twenty-Three:
The Last Sunrise

Two days later, the morning air was thick with an unusual, silent heaviness—as if the entire sky had lowered in sorrow, draping itself in a muted gray. The sea, usually bold and brimming with life, had transformed into a gentle whispering tide, its soft lapping against the dunes resembling a mournful sigh as if it, too, was grieving the loss of someone it had once lovingly embraced. The Jameson house stood eerily quiet, every room echoing the absence of laughter and joy. Sunlight filtered weakly through the drawn curtains, casting shadows that danced forlornly on the walls, emphasizing the emptiness inside.

The wedding robe, a delicate assemblage of lace and satin, still hung silently in the corner of the doorframe—a poignant reminder of dreams unfulfilled and love now lost. Naomi's bed had been made, and the covers pulled tight, but her absence pulsed through the room like a second heartbeat. Milo lay curled on the foot of the bed, unmoving, eyes watching the door.

Graham stood at the antique dresser, its polished surface reflecting the soft morning light filtering in through the sheer curtains. His hands trembled slightly as he lifted the delicate velvet box, its rich burgundy color a stark contrast to the muted tones of the room.

With a deep breath, he opened the lid, revealing the glint of Naomi's wedding rings nestled within the soft, velvety interior. The bands, a simple yet elegant design, caught the light, casting tiny sparkles around him. He pressed the cool metal to his lips, closing his eyes tightly as memories of their wedding day flooded his mind, the laughter, the vows, their dreams shared. After a moment of quiet reflection, he gently placed the rings into a small linen pouch, its texture soothing against his fingertips, and tied the drawstring with a subtle determination, as if securing the essence of their love within. He turned to his mother, who stood quietly behind him.

"She'll wear them," he said. "On her finger. Just as they belonged."

Jennifer nodded, her voice thick. "And the dress?"

Graham's eyes flicked to the chair where Naomi's light blue wedding dress had been folded. "She loved that dress. She glowed in it. I want her to rest in peace, as a bride."

At the quiet funeral home, the scent of lilies hung in the air, mingling with the faint hint of polished wood. Ruth gently smoothed the hem of the elegant navy dress draped over Naomi's still body, her fingers trembling slightly as she brushed a strand of chestnut hair away from her pale face. The room was filled with a soft, muted light, casting gentle shadows across the floor. Behind her, Thomas stood rigidly, his expression a mask of sorrow and disbelief, his eyes glassy and unfocused as they stared at the casket. He clutched the edge of the wooden pew, knuckles white, lost in a sea of memories that flooded him at the sight of Naomi, the vibrant laughter now silenced forever. The quiet atmosphere wrapped around them like a heavy blanket, amplifying their grief.

"She's beautiful," Ruth whispered.

"She always was," Thomas replied, voice breaking.

Pastor Eli Whitcomb arrived in a well-tailored gray suit, the fabric glinting softly in the afternoon light, with a well-worn Bible tucked securely beneath his arm. His face, marked by both age and compassion, bore the lines of years spent in service to his community. As he approached, he greeted each family member with a warm handshake, his grip firm yet gentle, offering comfort in the somber atmosphere. He lingered just a moment longer with Graham, his eyes reflecting a depth of understanding and empathy that spoke volumes as if to convey unspoken support during a difficult time.

"Would you like scripture at the graveside as well?" he asked gently.

Graham nodded. "Read everything. Read until the sky listens."

The service was held on the beach, just beyond the edge of the shoreline where Naomi had walked hundreds of times, her footprints a faint memory in the sand. Her casket, a pristine white adorned with delicate pale blue trim, rested gracefully beneath a small white canopy that fluttered gently in the ocean breeze. A single, carefully arranged bouquet of blue and white roses, their petals soft and fragrant, lay atop the lid, a poignant tribute to the beauty she brought into the world. The sound of gentle waves lapping against the shore provided a serene backdrop, as friends and family gathered, their faces reflecting a mixture of sorrow and love.

Layla stood a few paces away, her beloved violin cradled gently in her arms, its polished wood gleaming in the soft evening light. As the first guests began to trickle in, she drew the bow across the strings, filling the air with a haunting melody that mingled with the distant sound of waves lapping against the shore—mournful yet infused with an elegant grace that captivated everyone present.

Willow, clad in a delicate pale gray dress that flowed like a whisper around her ankles, turned to Beck with a mixture of anticipation and reassurance. Her fingers, slender and slightly trembling, reached for his hand, seeking comfort in his steady presence. Without a moment's hesitation, Beck took her hand in his, offering a firm yet gentle grip that spoke volumes of their silent connection amidst the gathering crowd. Chloe and Miles stood side by side, clutching a small jar of sea glass that Naomi had meticulously collected during her frequent beach strolls. Each piece, a unique blend of color and texture, shimmered softly in the sunlight, reflecting the memories of summer days spent searching for treasures along the shore.

Jennifer, with her arms wrapped tightly around both her sons, leaned in closer and whispered, "She brought us all together." Her voice was choked with emotion, yet there was a warmth in her tone that spoke of shared love and loss.

The crowd gathered was intentionally small—just family, a handful of close friends, and a couple of Naomi's former patients, who had quietly come to pay their respects. Their presence was a testament to the quiet yet profound impact Naomi had on their lives. The soft murmurs of their shared stories filled the air, mingling with the gentle rustling of leaves overhead, creating a serene atmosphere that honored the memory of a beloved soul.

Pastor Whitcomb stepped forward. His voice was

calm and rich, carrying across the breeze.

"Let not your heart be troubled: ye believe in God, believe also in me. In my Father's house are many mansions: if it were not so, I would have told you.
I go to prepare a place for you." (John 14:1–2)

He looked out at the group, then turned his gaze to Graham.

"She didn't fear the end," he said. "She welcomed peace because she had known true love. And in that love, she found her courage."

"The Lord is my shepherd; I shall not want. He maketh me to lie down in green pastures: he leadeth me beside the still waters. He restoreth my soul…" (Psalm 23)

Ruth pressed her trembling fingers against her lips, tears streaming down her cheeks like a steady rain. The weight of grief hung heavily in the air, wrapping around her like a thick fog. Beside her, Thomas sat in quiet despair, his shoulders quivering with muffled sobs, unable to find his voice amidst the overwhelming sorrow.

Pastor Whitcomb, with a solemn expression, gently closed his well-worn Bible, the leather cover creaking softly in the stillness of the chapel. He stepped forward and placed a reassuring hand on the polished casket, its surface gleaming under the soft light of the flickering candles.

"Let us pray," he said, his voice steady yet reverent, as he bowed his head, inviting those around him to join in a moment of collective mourning and reflection.

"Lord,
We thank You for the life of Naomi Jameson—
For her strength, her laughter, her compassion, and her heart.
For the love she gave freely and the lives she touched.

We lift up her soul to You now.
Wrap her in Your eternal light.
Let her walk streets of gold with peace in her heart.
And Lord, hold Graham. Hold him in the weight of this sorrow.
Give him the courage to live fully—
To grieve honestly, to remember deeply, to love again when the time is right.
May Naomi's life echo in every sunrise,
In every whispered breeze,
In every act of grace that follows.
In Jesus' name, we pray, Amen."

As he finished his last note, Layla's fingers danced over the keys once more, bringing forth a soft hymn that blended seamlessly with the gentle sea breeze. The melody floated through the air, filled with the salty scent of the ocean and the distant sounds of waves lapping against the shore, creating a serene atmosphere that enveloped everyone around. Sunlight sparkled on the water, casting shimmering reflections as Layla's music swelled, intertwining with the natural beauty of the moment.

After the service, the group walked in silence to a reception nearby—modest tables set up beneath white tents, food prepared by a local café that had once catered Naomi and Graham's engagement dinner. Graham remained quiet. He clutched the scrapbook in his lap—opened to the last page.

His eyes stayed on her handwriting, her swirled signature below the final entry: "Forever yours. Until I see you again."

Willow and Beck sat close beside him, their presence a comforting anchor amidst the turmoil. They exchanged quiet glances laden with understanding and support. Miles and Chloe moved around the room with quiet determination, refilling water glasses for everyone and anticipating needs without a word being spoken. Their unspoken gestures spoke volumes of their care and solidarity. Jennifer, her eyes glistening with unshed tears, gently wiped at her cheeks while recounting cherished memories of Naomi. She spoke of the radiant smile that could light up even the gloomiest of days, her love for zesty lemon cake that she would insist on baking every birthday, and the joyful image of Naomi dancing barefoot in her driveway, splashes of rainwater glittering around her like a magical spray as she twirled freely after a rainstorm. Each memory was a bittersweet reminder of the love and joy Naomi brought into their lives.

"She loved poetry," she whispered. "That's who she was."

Thomas stood at the edge of the beach, his gaze fixed on the waves crashing rhythmically against the shore, just beyond the lush green canopy of palm trees. The salty breeze tousled his hair as he finally broke the silence that hung in the air.

"It's mesmerizing, isn't it?" he said, his voice barely rising above the sound of surf and wind.

The golden light of the setting sun cast a warm glow on the scene, reflecting off the water's surface in a dance of shimmering colors.

"She gave us a summer," he said. "A hard one. A holy one."

As the day gently faded into evening, the golden sunlight gave way to a tapestry of pinks, oranges, and soft golds, casting a warm glow over the tranquil water. Graham stood alone at the water's edge, his silhouette a solitary figure against the shimmering surface. The sounds of laughter and chatter from the departing guests gradually receded, leaving behind a serene stillness that enveloped him like a comforting blanket. Milo, his loyal cat, was back home, curled up on his favorite spot on the couch, oblivious to the world outside.

In his pocket, Graham felt the familiar weight of Naomi's journal, its worn cover a testament to the countless memories and thoughts inscribed within. He pulled it out momentarily, running his fingers over its edges, recalling the delicate cursive that had poured out from her heart onto those pages. On his finger, the cool metal of his ring caught the fading light, a symbol of vows once spoken and promises now lingering in the air, heavy with unfulfilled dreams. He glanced skyward, seeking solace in the vibrant hues above, allowing the beauty of the moment to wash over him, even as a bittersweet ache settled deep in his chest.

And he whispered, "You were my sunrise. And my forever."

Made in the USA
Columbia, SC
11 June 2025